THE
Darkangel

The Darkangel Trilogy

The Darkangel

A Gathering of
Gargoyles

The Pearl of
the Soul of
the World

THE
Darkangel

MEREDITH ANN PIERCE

Volume I of
The Darkangel Trilogy

MAGIC CARPET BOOKS
HARCOURT, INC.
San Diego New York London

First Magic Carpet Books edition 1998
First published by Atlantic Monthly Press Books and Little, Brown and Company 1982

Magic Carpet Books is a registered trademark of Harcourt, Inc.

Library of Congress Cataloging-in-Publication Data
Pierce, Meredith Ann.
The darkangel/by Meredith Ann Pierce.
p. cm.—(The darkangel trilogy; v. 1)
Sequel: A gathering of gargoyles.
"Magic Carpet Books."
Summary: The servant girl Aeriel must choose between destroying her vampire master for his evil deeds or saving him for the sake of his beauty and the spark of goodness she has seen in him.
[1. Vampires—Fiction. 2. Fantasy.] I. Title. II. Series:
Pierce, Meredith Ann. Darkangel trilogy; v. 1.
PZ7.P61453Dar 1998
[Fic]—dc21   97-21253
ISBN 0-15-201768-2

Text set in Fournier
Designed by Kaelin Chappell
Printed in the United States of America
D E F G H I J K

YA Fic

To Joy, Carnell, and Dr. Green,
this dream of the Moon

Contents

ONE

The Steeps of Terrain

AERIEL RESTED THE BROAD BASKET AGAINST her hip and adjusted her kirtle. The steep climb she and her companion had been taking the last six hundred paces or so had caused the loose, flowing garment to twist around at the neck and fall askew.

"I have to rest," she said faintly, and not waiting for her companion's reply, sank down on the hard, grey brittlerock of the mountainside and set the empty basket down beside her.

It was cold up on the steeps, the air too thin to hold any heat. But Solstar was warm, a bare six hours from setting. Its white light streamed back at her from the eastern horizon, warm on her bare arms and neck and face, warming the broken rock shelf on which she sat.

Aeriel gazed out over the wide plain of Avaric,

fair as a pearl, bright as foxfire beneath the black, starry heavens. Oceanus hung, a swirl of blue and white, almost directly ahead of her. Below, she could see her village over to the right: tiny, far away, at the foot of the mountain and the edge of the plain.

"Come on," said Eoduin, digging her toe into Aeriel's backside. "We've still a way to go yet."

Aeriel sighed and got up, followed her companion. Eoduin was tall and slender, as befitted a person of lineage. After all, she was the daughter of the village syndic and her mother was half-sister to the satrap. She had a carriage about her, Aeriel observed wistfully, all self-sure and comely arrogance that came of living all her life in the largest house in the village, with sixteen different kirtles (think of it, sixteen! Aeriel had just two) and house servants.

Aeriel was one of these. She gazed longingly at her well-born mistress's hair, black as the heavens, with a blue sheen by earthlight. Eoduin's skin, pale and blue as breastmilk, had a subtle radiance that gleamed even in shadow. But Aeriel, slighter than her companion by a head, was boy-shaped still, her skin deeper-shaded: a wan rose-tan that even bleaching with lightning weed could not expunge. And her hair, thinner and finer than Eoduin's, was silvery yellow. Pretty enough by daylight, or lamplight—but it took on a hideous greenish cast, like unripe figs, by earthshine.

Aeriel sighed and scrambled up the slope after Eoduin, admiring the other's long-limbed stride, envying—but hopelessly—the unconscious ease with which the syndic's daughter held her basket slung over her back like a cloak. Aeriel knew that even when she herself began blooming into maidenhood (as Eoduin was blooming now), even then, she could never hope to match her mistress's proud grace.

After another hundred paces, Aeriel said, "We're getting awfully high."

Without turning around, her companion answered, "The summit's not much farther."

"I can't see the village anymore," said Aeriel. It was true. The turn they had just taken had led them around the mountain face a few degrees.

Eoduin laughed. "What are you afraid of?" she said, her sapphire eyes now mocking-merry. "Darkangels?" She stopped a moment to let Aeriel come up beside her. "You really do believe that old cradle tale Bomba was telling us," said Eoduin. "Don't you?"

Aeriel thought back on the strange, half-silly, half-deliciously exciting stories the bumbling old wife sometimes spun for her young charges at the distaff. She had told them one only a few hours before Aeriel and Eoduin had set out from the village to gather wedding flowers on the steeps— by way of a caution, Aeriel supposed, though this one had come out more muddled (and therefore ludicrous) than sobering.

Eoduin dropped her basket to the ground. Aeriel watched as she hunched her shoulders and screwed up her face in imitation of the old nurse's features. "The wraiths," she whispered, as if toothless. "The wraiths that roam the mountains, snatching bodies, causing landslides. Believe me...."

She wagged one claw-finger at Aeriel.

"Believe me, girl; I've seen them. Don't you go up high on those steeps, or you'll regret it— if you live to regret it." Aeriel bit her lip to suppress a smile. Eoduin always reduced her to helpless mirth. "And the vampyres!" Eoduin railed. "The icari: dozens of black wings and the faces of demons. One look'll turn you to stone, and then where'll you run, girl?"

The syndic's daughter began to stagger, worrying her hands and muttering.

"One'll swoop you away to his castle to make you his bride. And you know what the icari does with their brides, do you, girl?" Her voice had thinned from a low whisper to a faint, hysterical shriek. Aeriel wrapped her arms about her ribs and fought to hold back laughter. "They drinks up their souls!" Eoduin shrilled, then sank to her knees, gasping, "Oh, my heart, my poor heart...," exactly as Aeriel had seen her half-senile old nurse doing numberless times.

Aeriel gave up, laughed until she felt breathless and giddy, though the air on the high steeps was too thin for laughing properly or long. She felt a little sick with the altitude and had to sit down again, rest her forehead on her knees. Sobering now, she kept her face hidden. She did not want Eoduin moving on before she could regain her breath.

Unsmiling now, Aeriel thought about Bomba's stories and shook her head. No, it was not the tales of Bomba that had worried her—fat, good-natured Bomba—but Dirna's. Gaunt, furtive Dirna, who used to sit at the loom in the work-room a little distance from the others, staring off at nothing, her spare, withered fingers weaving by touch.

Her tales were of a different sort from Bomba's. Dirna whispered of dracgs and witches, gargoyles and specters—horrifying tales of death by drowning. Eoduin always laughed at them as she did at Bomba's simpleminded fables, but they made Aeriel shudder. Dirna never got muddled in her tellings: she spoke as if she knew.

Aeriel raised her head from her knees. Eoduin had risen and shaken off her guise. Pulling a few black strands of hair from her large, clear-blue eyes, she kicked her basket deftly downhill toward Aeriel, then nodded for her bondservant to follow as she strode gracefully up the path. Aeriel sighed shortly, collecting her mistress's basket along with her own, wished *she* had a servant to caddy for her whenever she grew tired of carrying.

"Cheer up, worry-wrinkle," Eoduin cried over one shoulder. "What vampyre would want you?"

Aeriel shook the frown from her face. "No, it's just that...," she began, starting after her companion and tripping. Balancing on the steep slope while clutching a basket in each hand was proving difficult. She scrambled to her feet, snatched up Eoduin's basket before it could roll away downslope like tumblebrush, and hurried up alongside her mistress again. "It's just that the sun will be down in a few hours, and..."

"Six!" cried Eoduin, laughing. "We've plenty of time before nightshade."

"Yes, but what if...?" Aeriel almost lost her

footing again on the smooth, crumbling rock, and
Eoduin pulled her to her feet without so much as
a glance or a pause in stride. Aeriel held to the
baskets. "But what if one of us gets hurt," she
continued, "or loses the way?"

"Don't you mean what if *you* get hurt?" asked
Eoduin, without rancor. "After all, you seem to
be the only one stumbling." She laughed and did
not offer to help carry. "But by the Pendarlon, if
I'd known you'd be so clumsy, I might have allowed more time."

Aeriel blushed and looked away. It was true:
she was clumsy, and beside her mistress's deft
grace, always felt doubly so. Her companion tilted
one shoulder in a shrug and glanced at Aeriel.

"Don't fear, little lameling. If you should twist
an ankle or knock yourself silly falling off a ledge,
I'll carry you *and* the baskets back in less time
than it's taken us getting this far."

Aeriel felt her color deepen, bit her lip against
retort. She wasn't lame—just awkward and unsure. Eoduin knew that. Aeriel's knuckles on the
basket whitened; she glanced at Eoduin. The syndic's daughter smiled at her carelessly. Aeriel's
eyes stung. These were the only times she ever
resented Eoduin, who used that hated name *lameling*, she realized, only to bait her. This time,

though, she seemingly meant no teasing by it. Perhaps she even intended it affectionately. Aeriel relaxed her hands and let her color fade.

"You needn't worry about the other, either," her companion was saying. Her tone was one of friendly tolerance. "I won't lose the way, and if you keep by me, you won't either."

Aeriel sighed and shoved her thoughts away, fell into step behind Eoduin again. The sun felt warm on Aeriel's back, and the shadows, whenever the path ducked behind boulder or ledge, were cold as well water. She dropped one basket from her hip as the trail grew narrower, let the light, bulky mesh of twined marshgrass bump along against her leg. They climbed.

She fell to watching the landscape, the lie of the rocks. She listened to the bell-thorn, silvery thin briars that tinkled like glass in the rare mountain wind. She watched the small, rose-colored lizards sunning themselves in the last hours of Solstar before crawling into their crags again to sleep for another long nightshade. She looked at the petrified bones in the rocks, bones of fishes, eels, and water plants left over from the time when the steeps had been nothing but flat mud bottom, and all the world a sea.

"Here, here are some," said Eoduin, halting so

abruptly Aeriel almost ran into her. Aeriel eyed the low-spread blossoming shrub at their feet. Eoduin gazed forward and gestured ahead. "And there are more up the slope."

They were near the pinnacle of the mountain. Aeriel could scarcely feel herself breathe. The sky was blacker here, the sun whiter, the Earth bluer, the stars brighter. When Aeriel looked down, she could see the light, luminous haze of atmosphere lying on the foothills, on the plain.

"You pick these," Eoduin was telling her, taking her own basket back. "I'll get the ones farther up."

It was difficult for Aeriel to hear her, the air was so thin. She obviously was shouting, but Aeriel, only a pace away, had trouble making out the more faintly spoken words. She nodded her reply.

"You brought a flask, didn't you?" demanded Eoduin, taking hold of the empty one she herself wore on a thong hung from her neck. It was a simple waterskin for desert travel, a couple of handspans long, made of white kid with an ivory stopper and beads of tinted bone. Aeriel nodded and tapped her own smaller, undecorated flask hanging from her neck.

"Good, then," cried Eoduin, softly, as from a

great distance. "Stay here, in sight—don't wander. And *don't spill any.*"

Aeriel nodded. Eoduin slung her basket over one shoulder and went on up the last, steepest twenty paces to the top. Aeriel watched her easy, surefooted ascent, her mistress's free hand resting lightly on rock or boulder from time to time to help her balance. Aeriel wished that she could have been born so long-limbed, so self-sure—so beautiful. She set her basket down and knelt beside the hornscrub, began gathering the flowers.

These hornflowers grew on a tiny, grey-silver bush which lived only on the highest steeps where the air was rare and perilously thin, not the slightest breeze ever stirring to disturb them. Each branch of the bush was covered with tiny, trumpet-shaped flowers: yellowish white, translucent as frost. Each trump was filled with a tiny drop of pale golden liquor, sweeter than ginger and richer than rum.

Aeriel pulled one blossom ever so gently from its twig. The trick was to gather them one by one, painstakingly, so that not a drop was spilled in either the picking or the pouring from flower to wineskin. The task was made doubly difficult by the flocks of tiny hummingswifts, no bigger than fireflies, that swarmed about the flowers and lip of the wineskin and could, between three or four of them, drink a horn dry before Aeriel could get the flower from bush to bottle. She shooed at them with one hand while keeping the other, holding the flower, perfectly steady.

Aeriel dropped the first, emptied trump into the mesh basket beside her and reached slowly for another bloom, and then another, and another. The motions became mechanical. Her back began to ache, and her legs felt stiff, but Aeriel ignored the pains, waved away the bothersome bee-birds and continued gathering.

A marriage was to take place in the village at sundown, dusk being the customary and proper time for weddings in Avaric. Eoduin, as eldest cousin to the bride, was pledged to bring the bridal cup of hornbloom nectar and garlands of the weddings trumps. But these could be harvested only a few hours before the marriage, the precious liquor and delicate blossoms so quickly spoiled.

It seemed to Aeriel as she poured the contents of another pale, trumpet-shaped flower into the goat-hide bottle, that the humming of the tiny swifts had grown rather louder, and shrill. She tossed the empty flower into the basket and ignored the sound to concentrate on carefully plucking another blossom. She imagined the preparations in the village: the decking of the streets with banners of white gauze, the bathing of the bride...

It occurred to Aeriel, then, that the sound she was hearing was not the angry whine of hummingswifts, but something else: a voice. Eoduin is calling me, she thought, as she pulled a flower away from the stalk. The pitch of the voice changed abruptly, intensified. Aeriel brought the hornbloom to the rim of the bottle. No, not calling anymore, she realized suddenly—screaming.

Aeriel dropped the flower, felt its droplet spill hot as a tear—no, hotter: hot as tallow; it burned her hand. She looked up the slope to where Eoduin was. The basket of wedding trumps lay overturned at Eoduin's feet. Her young mistress was standing mute now, looking up at the sky.

Then Aeriel saw wings, very near—great wings descending: a creature with more wings than she could count, all black, all beating fiercely. She felt a faint breeze against her cheek—for all the fury of those terrible wings, the air was too thin to carry more than a feeble gust.

They were jet, those wings, as deep as the sky, as black as Eoduin's hair—no, blacker, for they were dull, unoiled. They gave off no sheen in the light, no gleam to the eye. They drank up the light and diminished it: they were wings of pure shadow.

It seemed to Aeriel, as she watched that storm of darkness descend, that she discerned the figure of a man at its heart, a man dressed in some pale garment, a man of fair complexion—but the wings beat with such rapidity against the near-empty air that she could not make out his face.

The figure reached the mountaintop and alighted, but barely—his sandaled feet hardly touched the stone. Before him, Eoduin cried out in terror. Though Aeriel knelt not twenty paces from her, the sound was distant, as though it had traveled miles. He held out his arms to Eoduin, abruptly, as in command. Eoduin backed away. The darkangel stepped toward her. Aeriel could see only the vague white shimmer of his garment amid the dark fury of still-beating wings.

Eoduin whirled and began to run, down the slope toward Aeriel. She had not taken two steps before the vampyre had swooped and caught her. Aeriel heard Eoduin's piercing cry. The icarus' speed and Eoduin's weight bore them forward and down. His powerful wings thrashed the air. Aeriel bolted to her feet—too fast. Her legs, still from long sitting, would not bear her. The vampyre swooped overhead, so close Aeriel could have reached to touch him.

The world had reeled, and falling, she threw up her arms then, not to touch, but to ward off the cold, fleeting shade of those horrible wings. Her knees buckled. She felt her feet skid from under her. The darkangel was gaining altitude above her. She saw Eoduin still struggling in his arms, but could no longer hear her screams.

Aeriel felt her elbow strike the earth, and then her shoulder, as a dozen sharp, hard, rolling pebbles dug into her flesh. The ground was in motion beneath her, slipping, sliding. The icarus was already far away, a dark blot against the stars. She glimpsed the shadow of his dozen wings very small against Oceanus.

"Eoduin! Eoduin!" she started to cry; then her head struck ground with a sickening jolt. The back of her skull went numb. All the sky was white stars for a moment. Her scalp felt wet and warm. Then suddenly the brightness dimmed. "Eoduin," she heard herself breathe, barely, once, just before all the light in the world went out.

AERIEL LICKED HER LIPS AND BURNED her tongue on the sweetness of horn liquor. She was lying on hard, sloping ground. Jagged pebbles pressed into her back like great pus-pox, hurting her. She could feel the goatskin bottle on her chest and the warmth on her cheek and throat where it had splashed out, spilling. She was lying on the slope, her head lowest, her feet uphill from her: her toes were numb. All this she knew without opening her eyes.

She opened them slowly, saw the star-littered sky above through the slight glare of sun in her eyes. She tried to move and found it hard, very hard. Her head came away sticky from the ground with a soreness that made her feel sick and stupid. She got one elbow under her and propped herself up, gazed straight at Oceanus, a huge and constant blue with no shadow of wings across it now.

She said, "Eoduin," and wept, but she was too weak to weep much.

Her hand was cold. All her body was warm in the sun, but her left hand was cold: she looked at it presently and saw that the shadow of a boulder down the slope had crept across it. That frightened her. She snatched it from the shadow and sat up, twisted around—too quickly. Her temples pounded; she felt the blood running out of her head, and blotches of darkness wandered across the stars.

Solstar was setting. She could see it as her

vision cleared. It was barely three degrees above the horizon—and that would diminish as she descended the mountain. She twisted her head around the other way. The pain increased sharply at the sudden move. She could already see the shade of night across the desert to the west. She had two hours, maybe less, to get back to the village by nightfall. With the wedding procession about to begin, who would miss one little slave?

She chafed the leaden, cold-bitten hand in her lap and felt nothing. It was numb. She groped for the flask at her neck: yes, there was a little of the liquor left. She poured the bright liquid out onto her limp, waxy hand, then grimaced, rocked in pain as the heat soaked through the frostbite, burned to the bone and then to the marrow. As the heat diminished and was gone, color returned to her hand; she could move it.

She got to her knees and then to her feet, took a step, stumbled and fell. She got up again and started down the slope. The soreness in her head was mostly dull, but when she missed her footing and staggered, the pain stabbed. She clung to the rocks of the mountainside, to the scrubweed, to the crannies. She raked her arm on bell-thorn and scraped her knuckles raw when she slipped. Twice the winding trail crumbled beneath her feet and fell away down the mountainside like a tiny meteor shower. And always the sun sank lower as she descended the steep, and the shadows lengthened. The air grew warmer and thicker: her breathing eased.

Solstar had halfway sunk into the Sea-of-Dust by the time she heard the marriage hymns drifting up into the foothills on the soft plains wind. Strange. It seemed strange after the airless, muted steeps that here below, still a quarter-mile from the village, she could hear the singing so distinctly so far away. She listened to the words floating in the long, harsh twilight.

Farra atwei, farra atwei.
Narett, miri umni hardue....

Here in the foothills, just coming into the village, the path was much broader, smoother, less steep. She had come this way a dozen times: up to the spring to catch minnows, up to play in the caves and gather mushrooms, and just six hours past up into the mountains with Eoduin.

Aeriel grimaced with the pain of remembering. Eoduin had once pulled her out of one of those dark pools when she had slipped, pulled her out by the hair and pounded her on the back as they knelt, wet and shuddering, on the slick, steep bank until Aeriel had coughed up half a measure of bitter water and no more would come. That had been two years ago. Aeriel's head hurt, now, as she fled down the broad, smooth path by the caves toward the village. She did not want to think of Eoduin. She thought of the music instead.

> *Thyros idil temkin terral,*
> *Ma'amombi tembril ferral....*

The words were closer now, a little louder. She realized that she was in the village. The smooth, square, whitewashed adobe houses gleamed in the dying light of Solstar. Gathered gauze draped softly from their dark windows. The great street that ran east-west was a long corridor of light. The little north-south side streets were dark as death.

> *Anntuin dantuwyn tevangel hemb,*
> *Letsichel mirmichel gamberg an rend....*

She was passing the houses more quickly now: she could see the village square ahead, filled with people. Then suddenly she was among the people, who did not seem to notice her but went on with the singing, their eyes turned toward the half-gone sun. Pushing past them, she gave a cry to make them stop.

The hymn broke off raggedly in midverse. The syndic frowned from his place before the bride and groom. The bride in her new-woven sari glanced around. Behind her and the syndic, Aeriel saw Eoduin's mother, a thin-faced aristocrat with hair like night. Old Bomba swayed beside her, nodding off into sleep even as she stood. Aeriel stared at Bomba and the mother.

"Eoduin," she gasped, breathless.

The syndic, Eoduin's father, had been standing in shadow, came forward now into the glare. "Yes," he said, "where is she? The ceremony cannot be completed without the bridal cup." He eyed the flask still hanging from Aeriel's neck. "Has she sent you ahead with it?"

"She," said Aeriel. She could not catch her breath. "No, she..."

"Well, where is she, then?" demanded the syndic, pursing his fine lips. He gave an exasperated sigh. "How that girl can dawdle!" Turning back to Aeriel, his patience thinned. "Come, out with it, drudge, or I'll have you beaten."

"Gone!" cried Aeriel, marveling that even yet he did not understand. "The icarus," she faltered, "the one with wings..."

The syndic shook his head impatiently. "Are you gaming with me, drudge? Now where's my daughter, your mistress; where's Eoduin?"

Aeriel gazed at him and longed to faint. The syndic glared at her and would not listen. The townspeople all stood hushed now, staring. Her head felt light, ached; she felt her balance tip. She swayed and staggered. The syndic eyed her with sudden suspicion.

"Have you been tasting of those hornflowers, girl?"

Aeriel looked back at him with dull surprise. "I hit my head," she muttered, putting her hand to the sticky place behind and above her ear.

She felt something at once soft and stiff amid her tangled hair. She pulled it free from the mat of blood. It was a feather, black, a cubit long. It had been in her hair the whole time she had been coming down the mountain, and she had not known. Realization struck her with the coldness of shadow across strong light.

She shuddered once, staring at the thing. Her hand snapped open but the feather did not fall, stuck to the half-dried ooze on her palm. She shook her hand and still it clung, black and blood-damp; she could not bear to touch it or pull it free with her other hand.

The last ray of Solstar winked out, like a candle snuffed. The square was smothered in shadow. All was night. Aeriel could still see the vampyre's feather dimly, a black streak in the dark against the paleness of her flesh. No one moved toward her. No one stirred to help her. She gave a long, low cry of revulsion and despair, and swooned.

TWO

Vengeance

❧

"WHO WILL KILL THE VAMPYRE?" SAID
Aeriel softly, softly. The vehemence of her own
words surprised her. She was kneeling beside the
wide, low windows of the deserted alcove just off
the empty dyeing chamber. Night outside was
dark and still. Her mouth tasted like metal. She
had not known she could feel such bitterness.

She remembered waking hours, many hours after the sun had set, and seeing old Bomba along
with some others of the servant women murmuring over her or moving quietly about the darkened
chamber. Bomba had laid a cool, damp gauzecloth
on her forehead. Time passed. And then, she remembered Eoduin's mother, the syndic's wife,
shoving suddenly into the room, the women falling back deferentially, uncertainly before their
mistress, who came to stand over Aeriel, white-

faced and screaming: "So she is awake, now, is she—why wasn't I told? My daughter is dead because of you, worthless chattel!"

The woman's hair was disheveled, her thin cheeks tear-streaked, her garments rent with mourning. Her face above Aeriel looked like Eoduin's, only older. One long finger she leveled at Aeriel. "Why could you not have protected my daughter? You should have given your life for your mistress." The woman's breast heaved in a sob. "Why could the vampyre not have taken you instead of Eoduin?"

And then the sharp crack of the woman's hand against Aeriel's cheek, so sudden the tears sprang to her eyes. Startled murmurs from the servants, the syndic hurrying short-breathed into the chamber, pulling his wife away. "Come off, my dear. Such displays of grief are untowardly. You demean yourself before mere serving-women...." Then Bomba's great bulk bending over Aeriel again and fingering her stinging cheek gently with murmurs of "There, there, child. There."

Aeriel beside the alcove window stared out into the night. Since her recovery she had kept as far from Eoduin's mother as she might. She thought then of Eoduin, the mistress she had served almost since before she could walk. She recalled it vividly: the aristocrat's young doted-upon daughter pointing her out to her father at the slave fair twelve summers gone and begging him to buy that one, *that one*. Eoduin, who had been her constant companion since—more friend than mistress, though a proud and a high-handed friend. Her only friend.

Aeriel sighed bitterly. Now all things had changed. His daughter dead, the syndic planned to sell Aeriel soon—she had heard the servants' whispering in the halls—his wife demanded it. Aeriel thought of the provincial slave fairs in Orm: bids and shackles, confinements, blows. Here in the syndic's house, Eoduin had always protected her.

She would be sold northward, she was certain of it, deeper into the hills. Here at plain's edge, owned servants were sometimes treated with tolerance. But it was worse in the mountain heartlands: tales of slaves beaten or worked to death.... It chilled her, thinking of it. Aeriel closed her eyes to the dark outside. I cannot live without Eoduin, she thought, and I would rather die than brave the slave markets of Orm.

She pulled her tangled thoughts away from that, tried to think on other things. Already the village poets were beginning to sing of the syndic's hap-

less daughter, stolen away for the vampyre's bride.
Yet with all their singing and moaning and
murmuring in all the fortnight since, not one of
Eoduin's friends or kith had stirred a step to climb
the steeps again and confront her murderer. That
is not justice, Aeriel raged silently, in despair.

Holding the icarus' great black feather up before her face, she opened her eyes and stared at
it. Its dull darkness absorbed and nullified the
white and smoky lamplight. Without, the shade of
night, now three-quarters of a half-month old,
loomed blacker than birds' eyes. The white plain
of Avaric gleamed faintly in the pale blue light of
Oceanus.

"*Someone* must kill the vampyre," she breathed,
as to the feather, almost pleading; the quill's black
plumage stirred, "that Eoduin may be avenged."

"There is no vampyre," said Dirna gently, her
only companion in the small, empty room. She sat
behind Aeriel, combing out her hair—carefully in
back where her head was still tender.

"Then what is this?" demanded Aeriel, twisting
around. Her hair caught in the teeth of the comb
and pulled sharply. Catching Dirna's hand in hers,
she ran the older woman's long, leathery fingers
over the feather.

"I don't know," hissed Dirna quietly. Her

voice was always soft and sibilant, nothing like
Bomba's deep-sounding tones.

"Don't know?" insisted Aeriel. "What does it
feel like?"

The other sighed and groped for the little horn
comb hanging tangled in Aeriel's hair. "True, dear
one, it does resemble a feather—but it cannot be.
Perhaps it is a leaf or flower of some high mountain plant no one has ever seen before...."

"Dirna!" cried Aeriel.

Her fellow servant stared straight ahead and
said softly, assuredly, "There are no birds even
half so large. Birds are rose, or pale blue, or subtle
green. Yet you say this thing is black. There are
no black birds."

"It isn't from a bird," said Aeriel evenly.

"There are no vampyres," Dirna told her, with
infinite patience, "just as there are no mudlicks or
water witches."

Aeriel stared off across the room and held her
tongue. Dirna had been this way as long as she
had known her. Sometimes she wore an eerie look
that told she was in the mood for tales; then she
swore absolutely by the creatures of the dark. But
other times, her eyes seemed to clear a little, and
she scoffed at them all as nothing but mad minds'
wanderings.

The latter humor seemed to be on her now, and Aeriel despaired. Much as she shrank from Dirna's queerness, her calmer moods could be even more galling. She wished the other had not found her, come creeping into the little alcove where Aeriel had retreated to gaze out at the night; she wanted to be alone. She felt Dirna beginning to run through her fine yellow hair again.

"The air is thin up high on the steeps," she said. "Fatigue can trick your eyes. Perhaps a landslide, perhaps she fell—I don't know." The comb pricked and pulled at Aeriel's scalp. Dirna sighed. "You mustn't grieve, dearling. I know it wasn't your fault."

Aeriel stiffened and stared at her. Dirna seemed to be listening, but Aeriel saw no one in the outer chamber.

The older woman said softly, conspiratorially, "Eoduin was not the easiest mistress to serve." Dirna pulled a few of Aeriel's hairs from the comb. "But she admired you in a way—did you know it?—how you took her mother's every blow with never a sound. You know *she* used to fly into fits of tears if her father so much as slapped her...." Dirna fluttered her fingers to let the freed hairs fall. "She was even a bit jealous, I think. Did you sense that, my heart—resent it even—your mistress's jealousy?"

"What do you mean?" demanded Aeriel. Dirna's words astonished her. Eoduin jealous—and of her? Impossible. "I loved Eoduin."

"Say nothing to me," hissed Dirna softly, "and I will have nothing to tell." She found Aeriel's chin with her hand and turned it away to face straight ahead. She spoke almost beneath her breath. "Everyone believes you, you know—or else holds tongue. The syndic believes you, else he'd have had you beaten for the truth."

Aeriel felt the comb parting her hair.

"They went up into the steeps with candles—had you heard?—looking for the place. They didn't find anything, though—no wonder. You can't see a thing by earthlight and candles." The comb tugged at a tangle in Aeriel's hair. "They did find a few more of those leaves—feathers, whatever they are—so I heard. You were smart to strew them about. The body will have fallen all to ash by the time the sun's up."

Dirna's voice had hushed to a mutter. She laughed quietly, companionably.

"You're much cleverer than I took you for, little one. And there must be a deal more spirit in you than you've ever let show. Tell me; did you plan it, or just seize an opportunity? At sunrise, you can take me up and we'll hunt for the bones."

Aeriel stared at her. Her throat went tight. She wanted Bomba suddenly. She wished Dirna had never come. "You'll find no bones," she choked. "The only bones you'll find are the sea-things dead long years."

Dirna continued combing her hair, unconcerned. "Don't fear," she said. "You can trust me." The older woman's voice was full of pity. "I know that circumstance—the altitude, a sip of horn liquor: circumstances can make anyone a little mad."

Aeriel pulled hard away from her. "I didn't," she said. "You think I killed her and I didn't. It was the vampyre carried her away."

Dirna shook her head. "There is no vampyre, child."

"There is!" cried Aeriel. Her teeth were clenched. Outrage welled in her against the icarus, against Eoduin's faithless kith and friends, against Dirna and her soft, slippery words. The feather crumpled in her hand. "There is."

"Not so," said Dirna firmly. "Now let me comb your hair."

"No," said Aeriel, backing away.

"All is well," crooned Dirna with compassion.

"I understand how you must feel. Have I not told you? I killed someone dear to me once, too."

Aeriel looked at her with horror almost as deep as that she had felt on the mountain, and remembered one of the ghastly tales Dirna had once told her, all alone, in secret. It had been nothing like the silly, soothing old nurse tales of Bomba's. It was not even like the other ones Dirna herself had ever told, for *this* story, she had sworn utterly, had really happened—and to her.

Dirna sat, comb in hand, near where Aeriel stood, and gazed at nothing, her eyes bright and filmed over, blind. Aeriel shuddered and shrank from her. "What's wrong?" said Dirna, turning her high-held head a trace. "Come here."

"No," said Aeriel, falling back another step.

The madwoman reached for her. "Come here; I want to comb your hair."

"No," cried Aeriel and fled. The black feather fell from her hand as she ran through the empty dyeing room and then the crowded weavers' room. She tripped over a full basket of yarn, spilling the skeins across the dusty floor. Scrambling up, she fled the room, unheeding of the angry shouts that followed her.

She found Bomba in the spinning room, hunched over in one corner, nodding off to sleep.

Her great bone spindle lay fallen over on the floor, its fine wool thread beginning to unwind as her thick fingers relaxed. The other women spun and chatted, ignoring the old nurse.

"Bomba," cried Aeriel, falling down beside her. "Bomba."

Bomba sputtered and half-woke, sat a moment blinking, then reached her massive arm to enfold the frightened girl. "Hm, what's this, little one?" she murmured. "More nightmares?"

"It was Dirna," cried Aeriel. "She thinks... She said..."

Bomba woke a little more, gave a snort of disapproval. "Dirna, eh? You stay away from her, child—old tale-twister. She's a little fey, you know?"

Aeriel buried her face in the soft fold of Bomba's bosom and sobbed. "I will kill the vampyre," she choked, longing for Eoduin and hating her murderer. "I will kill him." Her whole body shook. She thought again of the syndic's wife: "Why could the vampyre not have taken you instead of Eoduin?" Now Dirna's words had made her feel even more deeply that it was somehow all her fault.

The old nurse clucked, patted and stroked her hair for a while. Gradually, Aeriel's weeping quieted. She clung to Bomba and felt no consolation. The old nurse settled herself a bit more comfortably, sighed and drifted off into sleep again. The women spun on, unconcerned.

THE CLIMB UP THE CLIFFS WAS STEEP AND Aeriel was out of breath, for she was hurrying. Solstar had been barely peering over the rim of the western deserts when she had slipped away from the others at their morning prayers in the courtyard of the syndic's house: praying to the Unknown-Nameless Ones, they who had first fallen from the sky in fire to quicken this, a then-dead world, the moon of Oceanus, into life. Little was known of them, and they were not much spoken of.

Aeriel quickened her pace along the brittle mountain trail. No one had seen her leave the village. She carried only the long-knife she had stolen from the kitchen and a small sack of provisions. She did not know how long she might have to wait, but she would wait—wait until the icarus came, or the food ran out and she died. Surely he will come, she thought, if only I wait long enough. He *must* come.

"Hear me, O Unknown-Nameless Ones," she panted, padding rapidly along the narrow, rising path. She had never prayed before, but she had heard the syndic do it, offering up the house prayers each morning and the village prayers each night. "Hear my words," prayed Aeriel. "Let there be justice for the killing of my mistress and my friend. Not any of her family seeks to avenge her...."

As I would, thought Aeriel, pausing for breath. Her head was spinning from her haste. Let them hear me for Eoduin's sake—I myself am of no consequence. The Unknown-Nameless Ones granted few prayers, she knew, and generally only personages of great importance dared petition them. She eyed the star-strewn sky uneasily, hoped fervently no blue-white lightning would dart down to silence her presumption. It was not courage that had prompted her to make this climb, only despair. The slave fairs would be held next day-month in Orm.

"Answer this entreaty of one small slave, O Ancient Ones," she cried into the thinning air, "and I care not what becomes of me after." What did her life matter anymore? Eoduin was dead. "I will go quiet into new slavery, or dedicate myself at Temple to your service, or spill my blood on the altar-cliffs in sacrifice to you—what you will."

All three prospects terrified her, but she made

herself speak the words. Surely the gods would have pity on one so desperate? The dark, vast sky above loomed empty but for stars. She gasped for breath and realized then that tears were streaking her cheeks. Her jaw hurt from having been clenched a long time, hard.

She scrubbed at the tears angrily, shoved away from the cliffside against which she had rested, and hurried on up the path. "I'm coward enough without weeping," she muttered. She gripped the long-knife tighter in one hand. But let him come, she prayed, silent again. Only let him come.

Solstar was a few degrees into the star-littered sky by the time she reached the summit. The air was thin, cold. There was no wind. She put her provisions down and knelt-sat on the hard, hot rock. The sun rose, slowly—half a degree every hour. The constellations turned, slowly. The waning Planet did not move, sat motionless in the heavens like a great, slow-blinking eye.

When the sun was four degrees into the sky, Aeriel ate a handful of bedchel seed and took a sip of water from the flask. When Solstar was six degrees above the plain, she ate again and stood up. Her legs were stiff and sore; one foot prickled numbly. She paced back and forth over the crumbling rock to get the circulation back. Then she sat down again and waited, dozed, ate, and waited again. He did not come.

The sun was sixteen hours into the heavens when she discovered the cracked mouth of her water flask had leaked half its contents into the thirsty rock. Solstar had climbed another twelve degrees when she drank the last of the water and threw the flask away. The sun was thirty-six degrees into the heavens when she ate the last bedchel seed. Her mouth felt tight and dusty, and she was hungry still. The stars wheeled slowly on. Her thirst and hunger grew until she felt dry and hollow as a reed. Solstar was halfway to its zenith when the vampyre came.

He came out of the northwest, as before, but this time she saw him from a long way off. At first she thought it was just hunger making the stars wink out occasionally, but no. She could see more clearly now that she concentrated, now that he was closer, that this small but growing shadow across the stars was more than a simple figment of her own fatigue. He was still far, and all she could make out clearly of him was the churning of his dozen wings against the dark sky and the faint, eerie glow of his garments.

He came very rapidly, as before. Aeriel stood up, shaking a little. For a moment, she was seized with the overriding desire to run, hide, escape lest he see her. No, let him pass, she almost prayed; let him fly on. But there was no mistaking that he must see her, now that she was standing, and no mistaking that his course was taking him directly to her.

She held the knife up in front of her in both her hands. He alighted on the cliff's edge, only paces from her. She felt the wind of his alighting and shuddered, but stood fast. His wings stilled, yet stayed spread. He draped and folded them about him in such a way she could see little of his figure and nothing of his face.

"You have been waiting for me," he said. His voice was startlingly quiet, clear, even beautiful— like a deep, full-ringing bell. The thinness of the air did not seem to affect it at all.

"Yes," said Aeriel, and her voice was nothing —a muted squeak. She gathered herself. "Yes, I have been waiting for you," she cried out boldly, and could barely hear the words herself.

"I knew that you would be here when I returned," the darkangel said.

"Then you would have done better not to have returned," she shouted, softly. She wondered what manner of hideous creature stood behind those wings.

"Do you mean to kill me?" his voice asked calmly, reasonably. The vampyre's wings rustled but did not part.

Hatred welled in Aeriel, and she cried, "Yes. You have taken Eoduin, and I will kill you for it."

"I chose her as my bride," he said. "It is a great honor."

"It is death," spat Aeriel, rage choking her.

She heard the vampyre sigh behind his wings. "After a fashion, I suppose, but that is small enough price."

"And how many now have you wrung the price from, icarus?" she demanded. "How many maidens have you stolen for brides?"

Silence followed for a moment, as though the darkangel were thinking.

"I think I have had twelve-and-one brides in as many years," he said, then laughed. "I am a young vampyre."

Aeriel gripped the haft of her long-blade tighter and started toward him.

"Stop," he cried, his voice of a sudden commanding and stern. "You have not the power, nor the will."

Then he opened his wings, and Aeriel found she could not move for wonder. Before her stood the most beautiful youth ever she had seen. His skin was pale and white as lightning, with a radiance that faintly lit the air. His eyes were clear and colorless as ice. His hair was long and silver, and about his throat he wore a chain: on fourteen of the links hung little vials of lead.

He was smiling at her slightly, a cruel smile that even in its cruelty was beautiful. Aeriel felt her knees buckling. The vampyre caught her as she fell and seized the knife from her. He clasped her to him. His body was colder than shadow, so cold she felt the warmth of her own body running away into his while his own cold invaded her. The air around him was bitter chill, smelled heavy and sweet as licorice. She felt his great wings buffeting around her suddenly, and realized they must be flying.

"Where are you taking me?" she tried to say, but he was holding her too tightly for her to speak, even to breathe. She felt the windless emptiness above the atmosphere, felt the vampyre's dozen wings straining in the void. We must be among the stars by this time, she thought vaguely, before the chill and airless dark intruded on her thoughts, and she lost consciousness.

HER FIRST AWARENESS WAS OF BEING able to breathe again. He had relaxed his grip. The atmosphere was rare yet, thin enough to make her gasp—but she could breathe. The darkangel's great wings still beat about her; she sensed the buoyancy of flight. And she was cold still, so very cold.

They were descending; she felt it—the rhythm of his wings had changed, and in the distance below, she heard a thin wailing, keening, almost screaming. It grew louder and more terrible as they drew near. Shriller it became, more raucous: hoots and shrieks and howls of hysterical laughter—until they were hovering in the midst of it. The buffeting of his wing-beats grew so fierce then that Aeriel half swooned. The screaming swelled and rose. The icarus touched down and stilled his wings. He let go of Aeriel and she dropped in a heap at his feet.

"Get up," he said.

Aeriel raised her head and looked around her. They were on the terrace of a tower, a tremendously high tower of cold grey stone: it sweated in the light. A spiral stair twisted up the central core a turn or two above the level of the terrace to the base of the pole where the standard flew.

It must have been woven of witch's breath, thought Aeriel, so light it was that even the seldom wind at such a height could lift it, send it streaming back from the pole in long furls.

Gargoyles sat on the battlements—lean they were and the same hideous damp grey as the stone. They looked at her with hollow eyes and rattled their silver chains. They had wings of bats or wings of birds, most of them, and licked their beaks or teeth with forked and double tongues. Two paced restlessly before their platforms; others whined or picked their claws, or groomed their mangy fur or feathers, or lizard skin, or scales.

The nearest one snapped at Aeriel. She drew away from them, pressed closer to the vampyre, but he moved off from her toward the hole in the floor where the spiral steps entered the tower.

"Come," he said. "They'll not attack you while you are with me, but you must not come here alone."

Aeriel looked first at him, at his beautiful bloodless face, his colorless eyes and long silver hair. She had never seen any living being so fair as the darkangel. She glanced back at the starved, ragged gargoyles. They had a sharp stench to them, like rotted cheese, or buttermilk. Aeriel could think of no creature foul enough to compare with them.

The icarus paused gracefully at the steps; all his moves were grace. "Do you come?"

Aeriel turned back to him. "I am to be your bride," she said, not questioning. The certainty of it overwhelmed her.

The darkangel looked at her then and laughed, a long, mocking laugh that sent the gargoyles into a screaming, chattering frenzy. "You?" he cried, and Aeriel's heart shrank, tightened like a knot beneath the bone of her breast. "You be *my* bride? By the Fair Witch, no. You're much too ugly."

Aeriel was silent for a long moment. "Then why have you brought me here?" she asked at last.

"You are to be my wives' tirewoman," he said, then turned and began to descend the stairs. Aeriel got to her feet but did not follow. The gargoyles shrieked and strained at their shackles. The vampyre halted after a moment and turned to her again. "Do you come, girl—what is the matter with you?"

"I am not to be your bride," said Aeriel.

The vampyre snorted; his lip curled with contempt. "And why in this world should I have to do with you? Certainly you can see your looks are hardly worthy of one such as I. Look at yourself—there is color to your skin, and one can see the blood in your veins. You are scant and scrawny; your hair is yellow, and those fig-green eyes... There, have I said enough?"

Aeriel looked at his flawless white skin that had no delicate tracery of blue veins beneath, his hair fine as filament, and platinum fair. Her own skin and hair were dark by contrast. The icarus continued: "However, despite that you are hideous to look at, I have brought you here—you can spin and weave, can you not?—to serve as my wives' tiring woman. Are you not delighted?" When Aeriel did not respond, the darkangel frowned and folded his arms. "Girl, I do not think you fully appreciate the honor I do you."

Aeriel came then, beneath the hard gaze of his disapproving eyes—the menace of his brooding made her flinch—and together they descended the tower into the keep.

THE CASTLE WAS IMMENSE, AND EMPTY. The vampyre led her through room on room of cold grey stone, rooms that contained nothing but an occasional piece of furniture—a carved alabaster couch beside a fine silk tapestry, perhaps, and that was all. The icarus looked about him with satisfaction. Aeriel gazed about her in dismay.

"Yes," he said. "They took most of it with them when they left. This used to be a king's palace, did you know it? But the king's son died young and his father grew old without an heir. Then I came when he was dying and the land had no champion to defend it, so the queen took her people far to the east, across the Sea-of-Dust to found a new kingdom. This is my palace now."

Aeriel followed the darkangel through the empty rooms and empty halls. "Have you many servants?" she made bold to say at last, for she hardly felt fear of him now, only a vast sense of insignificance.

"There is only you," he answered. "I had another tiring maid before you, but she tried to run away. She did not get far across the plain. I caught her by the hair and strangled her, then threw her to my gargoyles. If you try to leave here, I will do the same to you."

Aeriel nodded. After a time, she murmured faintly, "And what is to be my room, my lord?"

"Any room," he told her. "Find one that suits you and take it."

"And where are your apartments, lord?" she asked.

"I have none," he said. "There is only my bed-chamber, there, and it is locked."

He gestured to the right. Through an arched doorway, Aeriel saw another chamber, at the end of which stood a straight stair leading up to a landing. She caught only a glimpse of an ornately carved door, standing shut at the head of the stair, before the icarus turned down a hallway and Aeriel had to hurry to follow.

He nodded back over his shoulder toward his chamber door without turning. "I sleep but once a year."

He led her down corridors and stairwells, through the lower floors, the washing room—long dry and deserted, the storage rooms where no supplies were kept, and finally the kitchen of bare shelves where no herbs or onions hung drying from the ceiling beams.

"But what shall I eat?" cried Aeriel, dismayed.

The vampyre shrugged. "You must find your own food; the other ones always did. There is a garden—perhaps you will find something there. I, you may know, sup but once in a twelvemonth."

"On your wedding night," said Aeriel.

The darkangel stood fiddling with the leaden chain about his neck. "I have shown you enough of the castle," he announced suddenly. "Now you must meet my wives."

He led her up a winding stair, down a long narrow hall to a little door at the very end. It opened onto a tiny windowless room in which were twelve-and-one emaciated women. Some stood in corners or crouched, leaning back against the walls. Some crawled slowly on hands and knees; one sat and tore her hair and sobbed. Another paced, paced along a little of the far wall. All screamed and cowered at the entrance of the vampyre.

"Yes, they are a sight," he said to Ariel, "though they were all beautiful when I married them. I do not think the climate here agrees with them. Wives," he said, "this is your new servant. Do not encourage her to run away, or I shall have to kill her as I did the last."

The women looked at Aeriel with caverns where their eyes should have been. Their starved cheeks were translucent in the lamplight, the skin of their faces pulled so tight Aeriel could see the imprint of their teeth through their lips. Their arms looked like birds' legs—skin on bones with no flesh in between. They cringed; they trembled. One of them moaned: her voice was hollow. Their hair was all coarse and dry as blighted marshgrass. These are wraiths and not women, Aeriel thought suddenly—the soulless and undying dead.

"You must spin for them," the vampyre was saying, "and weave—nothing heavy, you understand. They are very fragile. Wool or even silk weights them down so they cannot walk, but must crawl about the floor like crippled beggars. I do not come to view them often, but when I do, I expect them to appear presentable."

"Not wool or silk," said Aeriel, watching the wraiths; "then what shall I weave?"

"You must find it yourself—something grows in the garden perhaps." He half-turned away, as if to leave.

"Which one of them is Eoduin?" said Aeriel, her voice fallen to a whisper as she realized one of these creatures must once have been her friend.

The darkangel shrugged. "Surely you do not expect me to remember which one is which?" He left her standing in the middle of the room.

Aeriel ran after him a pace or two. "Where are you going, my lord?" she cried.

He turned and said impatiently. "What business is that of yours? You are but a servant, and I have spent enough time on you."

"But...what if I should need to find you?" stammered Aeriel.

"Why should you need to find me?" said the vampyre. "Your duties do not concern me."

"But...," groped Aeriel, "I shall be all alone."

"Alone?" cried the icarus. "You have twelve mistresses and one." Then he turned and strode off down the hall, leaving Aeriel in the room with no windows, and the wraiths.

THREE

The Duarough

"WE WILL NOT HURT YOU," SAID ONE OF
the wraiths.

"We cannot," said another. "Most of us are too
weak to stand."

"It is the weight of these garments," another
said, or perhaps it was the first again. They all
moved about constantly, rocking or pacing, before
and behind her. Aeriel could not keep her eye on
them all. And all of them had the same face, save
that some were more or less withered than others.

"Our garments and our bones," another told
her.

"And the years."

"And the tears."

"The other one wove us garments she said
were of seedsilk," said one of the wraiths, "but

we are growing so thin that already they drag us down."

They moved a little closer, and Aeriel fell back until she pressed against the wall. A musty fragrance came from them, reminding her of ashes and root cellars. She watched the wraiths.

"You must weave us kirtles of finer stuff."

"Mouse-hair."

"Or birdsong."

"Or breath."

They looked at her with their hollows for eyes, and some of them nodded. Aeriel shrank away.

"Which one of you is Eoduin?" she whispered. Her voice would not stay steady otherwise.

"Oh, we have all lost our names by this time," they replied.

"Which one of you was the first to come here?"

The wraiths looked at one another in puzzlement. "We do not know," said one. "Our memories fade, then come again. None of us can now remember back much farther than a day-month, and there were always many of us a day-month ago."

Aeriel suppressed a shudder. "Why does he keep you here?"

"We keep ourselves," said the wraiths. "If we

wandered freely about this great castle, we would surely lose ourselves—what little there is left of ourselves to lose."

Aeriel grimaced at the creatures' closeness.

"Why are you afraid of us?" said another of the wraiths.

"What has he done to you?" cried Aeriel softly, able to keep her revulsion hidden no longer. "You were women once."

"True," said one.

"We were like you."

"But prettier."

"What has he done to you?" cried Aeriel again.

"Drunk up our blood."

"Stolen our souls."

"Torn out our hearts and thrown them to the gargoyles."

Aeriel turned away from them, groped for the door.

"Where are you going?" cried the wraiths.

"I," began Aeriel, finding the doorway with her hand.

"Do not leave us!"

"I . . . I must find the garden."

"We have no one to talk to," said one of the wraiths.

"You have each other," stammered Aeriel,

brushing away one slender mummy-hand that reached to catch a pleat of her kirtle and tug her back.

"We are all almost the same," sighed the wraiths. "Talking to each other is only a little more or less like talking to oneself."

"I—I must go," choked Aeriel, gathering her kirtle more closely about her against the delicate pulls and pinches of their hesitant, outreaching hands.

"Go," they told her, "but come back."

"I will come back," she heard herself promising—anything to be gone—and ran.

THE GARDEN LAY ON THE NORTH FACE OF the castle, above the cliffside, and had grown quite wild in the years since it had last been tended. Silvery spindle-grass threaded up through the pavement. Across the footpaths snaked sinewy creepers, their long, twining tendrils dotted by wine-scented blossoms with petals of gold. Elsewhere in the garden, the firethorn was in flower, and beside it the brittle-fruit stood blooming, its branches unladen as yet with sweet, crystalline drupes.

Aeriel wandered amid the flowers and the foliage, pausing now and again to peer through the fronds of white fig, or sort through the leaves of owl's feather wort in search of fruit, or seed, or nut—but there were none. And slowly she began to wonder whether this might not be a garden arrested in midseason: where everything flowered but nothing came to fruit, nor perhaps ever would wither and die.

Aeriel was hungry. Solstar had climbed a dozen degrees in the black, starry heavens since she had last eaten, and more than that since she had last tasted water. The nectarine scents of the flowers made her stomach twist with hunger. Her throat was close and dry. She had begun to feel lightheaded, dizzy.

She spotted a statue in the sunlight only a few paces from her, a little man about three feet high. He had a quizzical face and a long, twining beard. Aeriel approached the stone figure, leaned against it for support—but he was not a statue, she discovered. Only a moment after her shadow fell across him, he slowly blinked, then pursed his lips and stretched.

"Well, Merciful Darkness, girl," he sighed. "I thought you'd never—*don't* move!" he cried as Aeriel leapt back in surprise. As he said it, he jumped with her so that he remained in her shadow. "Now keep your wits, girl," he continued quickly. "I couldn't hurt you if I wanted, and I can be of help to you if you'll have me."

"Who are you?" said Aeriel hesitantly, more intrigued than frightened.

"You may call me Talb," the little man said with a bow, still careful to remain in her shadow. "It is not my name, but then, one must be careful just whom one hands one's name out to these days. And who, may I inquire, are you?"

"My name is Aeriel," she replied. "I come from the foot of the steeps of Terrain."

"That far?" said the little man. "Well, he must have brought you, then—not one of his new brides, I hope? But no, you're not wasted enough, and it's too soon, besides. *May* we stand out of the sun, mistress?" Here the little man's tone grew petulant. "It's rather awkward trying to stand here in your shadow when you keep bending and cocking your head to peer at me. Perhaps the songbriar over there...?"

He gestured and Aeriel nodded. They walked carefully to the shade of the leafy songbriar and sat down on the grassy limerock.

"You're his new maid, I suppose," said the little man, straightening the sleeves of his robe. The air about him smelled like old parchment and calf.

"I'm to spin," said Aeriel, "for his wives."

"Oh," said the other with some distaste. "Those awful wraiths. They wail, did you know? Worse than the gargoyles. I've tried talking to them, once or twice—witless things. I think their brainpans must be empty."

Aeriel looked at him. "I find them pitiable," she said, trying hard to put down her repulsion. She had promised to go back. "Grotesque, perhaps, but it's not their fault."

"Oh, without a doubt, without a doubt," the little man agreed, "but not much company."

Aeriel looked off across the garden. "Who... I mean, *what* are you," she asked him, "and from where do you come?"

The little man's tangled eyebrows rose. "I'm a duarough," he cried, almost indignant; "can't you tell? I come from the ground, from the caves under the ground, from the great caves, from the jeweled caverns. I was treasurer to the late king in my time, kept the vast storehouses brimming with jewels—all empty now. There is only the lime crystal left in the caves, though that is lovely...." His voice trailed off and his little stone-grey eyes grew moist remembering.

"What were you doing in the garden?" Aeriel asked him in a moment, when he did not continue. "That is, why were you standing so still?" She was afraid to admit she had taken him for a statue.

"Hm?" said her companion, coming out of his thoughts. "Oh, yes, well—I'm a duarough, as I said. Are you sure you have not heard of us? We do well enough by dark, or starlight, or earthlight, or even lamplight—but the light of Solstar blinds us, halts us in midstep, turns us to stone, you might say; we can't look away." He chuckled softly, stretched again, and yawned. "I had just come out in the predawn for a bit of fresh air— but I'm afraid I dozed, and the sunrise caught me. Marry, I was glad when you stumbled across me! I was afraid I should have to stand there all day-month till sunset, staring into that wretched star."

Aeriel felt her hunger returning as her initial surprise faded. "You said you could help me," she said in a moment.

"Ah, yes, and so I can," said the duarough, "so I can. I tried to help the one before you, but she wouldn't listen. At first she was of good heart and as gay as could be expected. But the day-months grew long, and she began to look weary as the wraiths—hollow-cheeked and hollow-eyed." The little man sighed and shook his head. "She knew she mustn't run away. But she kept straying to the steps in the cliff face that lead down to the plain. One day she took them, poor thing—didn't get

very far. The gargoyles saw her escaping almost
at once and raised the alarum, dreadful sound!"
The duarough looked at Aeriel. "I suppose that is
why he brought you here, to replace her."

"Please," said Aeriel; she was feeling faint. "Is
there any food in this garden?"

"Ah, food!" her companion cried, as if suddenly remembering himself. "Of course. No,
there's no food in this place, but if you'll follow,
I'll take you to my caves, where there's food and
in plenty."

THE CAVERNS WERE VAST, GREAT HOL-
lows in the bedrock on which the castle stood.
They stretched on in a winding chain far beyond
the limit of the pale rushlight the duarough held
up high. A gleaming river ran out of the endless
chain of caverns to the left, through the high-
ceilinged natural hall into which they were emerging, and away down to the right, where Aeriel
could hear the water's splashing echoed back
through a myriad of long vaulted chambers.

"Where does it lead?" said Aeriel.

"Miles and miles," the duarough replied. "Oh,
heavens, child, I've never had the time to follow—all the way to eternity for all I know." He
hopped off the last step of the tunnel of stairs they

had taken down into the earth from the garden. "Now come along," he said; "we shall have to wade."

He stepped out onto the sandy bank and Aeriel followed. The sand lay smooth and white as sawdust, felt at the same time soft and gritty. The water was warm, the current swift but not treacherous. And Aeriel realized its light was not merely the reflection of the duarough's torch, but an actual property of the river. Aeriel stopped in midstream, cupped her hands to the water and brought it to her lips. There was a taste of minerals to it, vaguely saline, and a soothing, almost herbal fragrance. It settled her stomach and steadied her. She drank again and followed the duarough to the opposite bank.

He led her along the cavern wall then, for a little way. It was of smooth white limestone and sprang up only a pace or two from the riverbank. They came to a place where the wall doubled back a step (though the river did not) before running on, and there in the shadow of that narrow niche was an ivory door—invisible until the duarough held up his rushlight to it and pushed it aside. It gave easily.

There was a narrow passage for a few steps, and then a great chamber of white limestone bare of anything but a small heap of sticks in the middle. They burned merrily—leapt in white flame—being dry and grey as desert driftwood. The duarough went forward into the chamber—his rush was almost burnt out—and tossed it into the little blaze.

"Come, girl," said the duarough. "Sit by the fire and rest while I fetch us some food—for I have not eaten in as long as you, probably longer."

Then he hobbled off across the room—his legs were very short—and disappeared through a door in the wall, one Aeriel had not noticed before. It was, like the other, carefully concealed by the shadows and unevenness of the wall. She sat by the fire, watching the pungent woodsmoke rise to the ceiling in a thin, white line, where it pooled and filled the little pocks and pockets there. Aeriel had never seen a wood fire before. The people in her village burned oil in lamps and jars, or candles.

Presently, she heard the duarough returning on the other side of the little door, ambling along and mumbling a quiet tune to himself. His arms were laden with fruits and berries. He knelt down beside the fire and spread them out. Aeriel sat staring at the quantity and variety of it all.

"Well, eat," the duarough said. "And you had best be quick, or I shall eat it all myself."

Then he immediately fell to and Aeriel followed. There were quinces and lemons and pale mauve citrons, pearl nuts and fanworts and pumpkins of gold. There was bitter-gummed saproot and taproot of cane, and squat milky mushrooms sweeter than nutmeat and smoother than curd. There were fish, too, dead ones. Aeriel was astonished.

"You eat them?" she asked the duarough. "Fish?"

"Certainly, daughter," the duarough replied, offering her some. "That is what they are for."

Aeriel tasted a bit of the moist white flesh. It was warm and tender on her tongue. "But they are dead," said Aeriel. "How is it their bodies have not fallen into ash?"

"Hm?" mumbled the duarough, munching on almonds now. "Oh, the cooking does that."

Aeriel ate of the little man's provender until no more was left, for the duarough, it seemed, was fully as hungry as she. She realized that, after all, he had not eaten since before sunrise—though since he had been dead stone most of the while, not living flesh, she was surprised he should have developed such an appetite. At any rate, it made no matter, for between them, they both had quite enough.

"Where does all this come from?" asked Aeriel when they were done.

Her host was busy collecting the leavings of their feast. "The food? From the caves, from the stream," he said, looking up. "Here is life."

"The water," said Aeriel, "it's warm. Where does it come from?"

"From the ground, daughter, from the earth."

Aeriel felt a frown creasing her brow. "But it's warm," she said. "Water out of the ground is cold."

The duarough nodded. "Aye, still water, dead water. But this is real water, girl. It runs and glows and bubbles with life."

"But so much of it," answered Aeriel, thinking of the depth and breadth of the stream.

"Much!" her companion cried. "That's barely a trickle. Ah, if you could have seen the caves of Aiderlan as I did in my childhood." He sighed. "Water still fell from the sky in my youth, and swelled the rivers. We called it rain."

"From the sky?" said Aeriel, for wonder. "How long ago were the days of your youth?"

The duarough sighed again. "A dozen thousand

day-months past," he said and fell silent for a little space. Presently he glanced at Aeriel again. "Well, where did you think the water went when the seas receded and the land arose?" He laughed a little, sadly. "Underground, daughter, underground. Here is life."

Aeriel swallowed the last quince seed, smiled a little, timidly, said nothing.

"Come," the duarough said, pocketing the last of the scraps, "are you rested? I want to show you the caves."

"Now this," the duarough said, rising from beside the little fire where he and Aeriel had just had their repast. He dusted off the backside of his robe, then his hands. "This used to be the great treasure room. It's quite empty, of course, now—they took it all with them when the queen and her people removed across the Sea-of-Dust to Esternesse. All, that is, except the blade adamantine, which was lost in these caverns long ago. He still comes down here looking for it sometimes."

"Who?" said Aeriel, rising with him now from the hard lime floor.

"The vampyre, of course," the duarough replied. "Surely you know the prophecy—no? By the Wardens-of-the-World! where have you lived all your life, child? That only by the hoof of the starhorse and the edge adamant may he be undone, and his six brethren with him. They are invulnerable to blades of mortals, but the blade adamantine was not forged in this world by mortals, but by the Ancestors, the Ancients, the Heaven-born of Oceanus."

He eyed Aeriel closely then, and she gazed back at him with a frown of puzzlement.

"Child, you've never heard of the Heaven-born?"

Aeriel shook her head. "Only in whispers, and oaths," she answered. "And prayers." She remembered her own desperate petition to the Unknown-Nameless Ones as she had ascended the steeps long ago that dawn, and blushed now to think of her presumption. She did not even know so much about them as their names.

"Not heard of the Heaven-born?" the duarough snorted. "Why, it was they who grafted life onto the land. This planet was a dead world before they came. They unlocked the water from the ground, created the atmosphere and bound it lest it bleed off into the heavens. They found the old seeds lying dormant and revived them, then bred their own herbs with them to create new plants for this world."

He gestured about him as if to take in the whole planet. Aeriel stared at him in wonder.

"They brought the animals," he said, "newly created for this world and us—even us they made, daughter, to farm the land and mine the caves." He folded his arms then, shook his head. "They themselves lived in domed cities in the desert, for the air was too thin for them to breathe long and live." He sighed. "They were our creators and our guides, for they were very wise. But they are all gone now. Great wars on their homeland destroyed them—or perhaps it was only their ships they lost, and so could no longer plunge across deep heaven from their far world of blue water and cloud."

Aeriel gazed at him and felt weak, marveling at his knowledge. He shrugged a little and smiled ever so slightly.

"Perhaps we shall yet live to see them come again." He sighed. "But enough of this. The caves. Come with me."

He bent to lift a piece of burning driftwood from the fire and led her out of the great storehouse through the hidden door he had taken to fetch the food. Aeriel followed him through a long series of lesser chambers that had been, the duarough said, storehouses of the greatest treasures: rooms unknown to any but the king and queen of the castle and their treasurer. And always from their left as they walked came the sound of running water.

"If ever you get lost in these caves," her guide informed her, "just follow the water and you'll find your way out."

Presently the tunnel of rooms bore right a little, and Aeriel could hear the water ahead of them as well as from the left. They came to the last room, which seemed to end with no door to a chamber beyond. But the duarough walked on without pause to the far corner, though it was no smooth, straight joining of planes, for all the rooms were rounded and irregular in shape, and slipped through a little door that Aeriel could not see until she was almost upon it.

They emerged onto the sandy bank of the river, upstream from where they had been. Aeriel turned and started down along the bank for the stairs up to the garden, the last step of which she could just make out around the far bend, but the duarough turned upstream.

"Come along," he said. "There is a way out closer than that."

Aeriel turned around and followed him. "May I come down to these caves sometimes?" she inquired. "They are very beautiful—far more beautiful than the icarus' castle...."

"I should say," the duarough replied, "and by much. Here there is life, and that cold tour up there holds only death and death. And as for the coming down sometimes, of a certain you may—you will have to, if you want to eat. And I shall welcome you. I haven't had someone to talk to for ages." They waded back across the stream. "The other one, the one before you," the duarough continued, "she stopped talking after a while. Those loathsome wraiths did it to her, I'm sure. Poor dear, she went quite mad as they in the end. Ah, here we are."

He had reached a narrow stair, which, instead of carving a tunnel into the rock as the garden stair had done, was cut into the side of the rock face, and ascended the wall in a slippery, uneven row of steps. The duarough motioned her up the stair ahead of him. The white torchlight wavered and danced behind her now as she ascended into the shadows where the light of the river barely reached.

"Where does this lead?" she asked the duarough.

"Up to the castle," he said. "It opens into the
corridor by the servants' quarters. There are some
nice little rooms about. You might like to choose
one of them as your own—it is away from the
noise of the gargoyles and the wraiths when they
decide to start moaning.... Oh, I almost forgot."

Aeriel paused on the stair and half-turned, for
her torchbearer had stopped and was now rum-
maging in the many folds of his full grey robe.

"Ah," he said, and drew from his pocket a little
object of gold—not the white zinc-gold or pale
electrum her people usually called gold—but true
fallow gold, more tawny than anything Aeriel had
ever seen before. "You'll need this if you intend
to spin for the wraiths," said the duarough and
handed it to her. "Your spindle."

It was indeed a spindle—tiny enough to cup in
the hand, but weighty as lead. Aeriel held it in
her hands and wondered at the delicacy of its
make.

"One of the few trinkets the queen left behind,"
he informed her.

"But," said Aeriel at last, "how shall I use it?
I have found nothing as yet to spin."

"Nor will you," the duarough said, "if you

mean to search in the garden or the castle for flaxsilk or fiber: there is none. No, what you spin must be of yourself...."

"I have not hair enough on all my head to make even one kirtle...," stammered Aeriel, and at this the duarough laughed—a surprisingly hearty, deep-throated laugh for such a little man.

"I can see that you are not acquainted with the singular properties of this golden spindle," he said after a moment, regaining himself. "This spindle spins from the heart, child—joy, sorrow, anger, hate. Whatever you feel in your heart this spindle will spin. The last one, the one before you, she spun on it pity and loathing—that was all she could manage in the company of those dreadful wraiths, and I can little blame her. But such garments fall to pieces in only scant time, and they are too heavy for the wraiths to bear. No, I think you must find something else to spin on this spindle, daughter." He gestured up the stairs. "Go along now, girl. The door to the castle is only a few steps up."

"But what am I to spin if not pity and loathing?" said Aeriel, astonished. "What else can one feel for such poor creatures?" Then, almost to herself, "And how am I to make thread of my heart's feeling—any feeling—at all?"

But the duarough had already turned and started down the steps. "Oh, I've no idea, child," he called over one shoulder. "We duaroughs are miners and scholars, not spinners. You must learn in your own way and in your own time how to use it, as well as what to spin."

And Aeriel was left standing, quite bewildered, with the golden spindle in one hand, until she realized she had best turn and find the door into the castle quickly, before the duarough and his light receded too far down the steps.

FOUR

A Spindle of Fallow Gold

LEARNING TO USE THE SPINDLE PROVED long and difficult. Aeriel spent hours in her chamber—she had found a small, bare room in the servants' quarters to serve as hers—sitting with the spindle, going through the motions of back-spinning a few threads of nonexistent fiber, securing them with a half-hitch, then giving the spindle a twist to set it spinning and letting it drop, just as she had done with her spindle of ram's horn at home. Nothing availed. Instead of producing thread on which to hang and twist, the golden spindle inevitably dropped to the floor with a clear, heavy clink and sat there turning like a top until it fell over. Try as she might, Aeriel could not master its mechanism. The day-months passed.

The wraiths, of course, were no help. She went to visit them often, as promised, but they were so horribly thin and dreary, and complained so bitterly at the weight of their coarse, drab garments, that she could bear them for not longer than an hour at a time.

The gargoyles, too, she took to visiting, though she was careful never to approach close enough to be scratched or bitten. She brought them fish and mushrooms that she had gathered in the caves—they looked so starved and their eyes were filled with such pain that she could scarcely help but feel pity for them. After she had come to them several times, they began to look for her—to yap and yelp the moment they heard her step on the tower stairs. Gradually, as the day-months passed, they grew less bony, even sleek. Their eyes lost their wild glaze, and they ceased to howl and shriek so terribly on the long fortnights.

And then suddenly Aeriel discovered the working of the spindle. She had been practicing, striving with it, trying for hours to cajole it into producing a thread. This it had stubbornly refused to do. And slowly, as she went through the motions of spinning, without thread, she fell into a kind of daydream, remembering her first spinning lesson at the age of four, in the spinning room among the other women—spinning their white wool with absentminded ease.

Bomba had put the ram's-horn spindle into her hands, shown her how to draw and twist back the wether's wool into the beginnings of a thread, how to wrap it around the base and secure it at the topnotch in the shaft, then let the spindle fall and turn while she drew the wool in thin tufts through her fingers and let them twist away as the spool of ram's horn dropped down, slowly down—it seemed an eternity—until it touched the ground with a click and fell over.

But the sound Aeriel heard now, as she stood in her room in the vampyre's castle, was not the soft click of old bone on hard-packed earth, but the bright clink of gold on stone. She looked down, and there at her feet lay the spindle, still turning idly, with a coarse white thread twisting up from the shaft. Quickly, before she could lose the knack, Aeriel snatched up the spindle, wound the thread, and let the golden spool drop. The thread did not break, continued to form, though it was thick and ragged as a gasp.

"It must be amazement," thought Aeriel, "that I am spinning, for I am amazed to be spinning at all."

After that, she took the spindle with her when she visited the wraiths, and spun there. At first she could find only pity to spin for them—a coarse, dull thread like the garments they wore. And when, after a few hours in the wraiths' company, she could stand them no more, sometimes the thread turned to woolly loathing, sticky and stinging as a bruised nettle stem. Then she would leave them and go down to the caves to bathe in the warm river or talk to the duarough. And after a while, she would go back to the wraiths and take up the spindle again, twisting a thick thread of coarse, dull pity out of the air. The day-months passed.

And then one day it all changed. The wraiths had become familiar to her now. Though their bodies were even thinner than when she first had seen them, their pitifully dull wits actually seemed to have improved slightly as she spent time with them, talked to them. Glimmerings of memory came to them now, though when Aeriel pressed them, none were often able to distinguish between glimpses of their own past lives and snatches recounted by a sister wraith. Aeriel still could not determine which of them was Eoduin, indeed, was not entirely sure she could have borne the knowing.

Gradually, though, she was coming to tolerate, then even take with good humor, the whining whispers of her charges (despite the vampyre's

words, they were not really mistresses), their nag-
ging insistence that the thread she was spinning
was too heavy and coarse. She had run out of
loathing, and though they were painfully eager for
attention, she tried not to pity them. And one day
while she sat spinning, she found the thread passing through her fingers was growing thinner, and
finer; then the coarseness went out of it completely
of a sudden, and she realized she was spinning
patience now—and love followed fast behind.

Whereas an ounce of pity had spun only a skein
of thread, and loathing even less, a drop of charity
made a thread so fine and long that she had not
yet reached the end of it. And whereas the spinning of pity and loathing exhausted her after only
a few hours' work, charity and patience was the
easiest spinning she had ever done. Soon she was
weaving kirtles for the wraiths on an old hand
loom she had found abandoned in one corner of
the cellar: the work was light and taxed her not
at all.

Once, after several day-months had passed
(three or four; she did not count them), she saw
through a window the darkangel standing on the
ramparts of a balcony that jutted from the castle
overlooking the garden. She stopped to look at
him. It was the first time she had seen him in a

long turn of stars, perhaps even since the last day-month. The icarus stood gazing out over the plain. His wings sloped down from his shoulders like a thick cape of black velvet that swallowed the light of Solstar and gave none of it back in a sheen. His face was fair as limestone, perfectly immobile—as though chiseled of stone—but his colorless eyes roved aimlessly over the barren landscape.

He turned suddenly, and saw her. Startled, Aeriel drew back from the window, but he called to her—not by name; she did not think she had ever told it to him: "You, girl." And she went out to him—for when he looked at her straight on, his clear eyes meeting hers, her strength failed her. She could do no other than to obey him. He turned away from her and gazed again over the plain. "Someone has been feeding my gargoyles," he said. "Was it you?"

"Yes, my lord," she answered softly.

"I did not give you permission," he said shortly, still looking out over the land.

"No, my lord," she said.

"Why?" demanded the vampyre, still not looking at her, "why did you do it?"

"They were so hungry, my lord," said Aeriel.

He looked at her now, and, seeing again the cold beauty of his face, Aeriel felt weak.

"I like them kept lean," he said. "They make better watchdogs then."

It was not until he looked away that Aeriel found her tongue. "Their eyes will be sharper and their ears the keener if they are not distracted by hunger...," she began.

"Do you propose to argue with me?" snapped the icarus.

"No, my lord," said Aeriel softly.

The vampyre drummed the fingers of one perfect white hand on the battlements. They gleamed slightly, like lambent Avaric, against the dull, dark stone. "Tell me, how did you manage not to be killed by them?"

"Their chains are not long enough to let them come near me if I stand against the stair."

The darkangel nodded, then turned to glance at her over one night-winged shoulder. "You knew this before you went up?"

She shook her head, for she could not speak while he watched her.

"Then why did you go up?" he asked her.

"They needed someone to feed them," she stammered as his eyes wandered.

"They would have killed you if they could," said the vampyre.

She answered, "Yes."

"Then why?" he said, with real curiosity now. "Why did you go up?"

Said Aeriel, "They needed me."

The darkangel shook his head then and laughed. "I suppose I should kill you," he said idly at last, "I did forbid you to go up on the tower—but I shall not. You are interesting. Not one of my servants was ever brave enough to go up amongst the gargoyles before, much less disobey me." He shook his head, frowned very slightly. "Strange. You do not look brave."

He eyed her then as though he expected some answer. She looked away. "I am not brave, my lord."

He laughed again. "Perhaps not. Perhaps you are only stupid. No matter. Henceforth you shall feed my gargoyles as well as attend my wives."

He paused then, expecting another reply, and Aeriel murmured, "You honor me, my lord."

"But keep them lean," he said, with a sudden severity. "If ever I discover them growing fat and sleepy, you shall be their last meal for a long twelvemonth."

With that he strode away from her and disappeared into the castle. Aeriel leaned against the terrace wall for many moments after, waiting for her heart to steady and her strength to return.

AS THE DAY-MONTHS WORE ON, AERIEL became aware that the vampyre was growing more restless, pacing the castle and muttering. "He is growing hungry," said the wraiths; their wits gradually were sharpening. Eight of them had new kirtles now. "Half the year is up," the duarough told her, "and in a few months' time, he will fly in search of another bride." Aeriel often caught glimpses of him, prowling through the keep.

Sometimes he caught the little silver bats that flew about the towers after dark in search of tiny moths and millers; the icarus caught the bats and broke their wings. This Aeriel knew, for sometimes she came upon them starved to death on the walks about the keep, or fluttering helplessly across the floor of some empty castle room.

One day in the garden she came upon him. Cupped in his hands he held some tiny, struggling creature. A bat, she realized in a moment. It was a bat. He had broken only one of its wings and was tossing it into the air to watch it flutter back to earth in a frantic spiral. Aeriel could just make out its high, thin twittering on the very limit of her hearing. Before she could think, she found herself running forward.

"Stop," she cried out. "Stop!"

The vampyre ignored her. The bat struck the cobbles of the walk and ceased to move. The icarus nudged it tentatively with one sandaled foot, then picked it up by its crumpled wing and shook it. The bat did not stir. Aeriel stood watching.

"Don't," she cried. "Please don't throw it up again. It's stunned. You'll kill it...."

The vampyre laid the bat down on the garden wall long enough to look at her. Her voice trailed away and died. The icarus eyed her a long moment with his eyes clear and colorless as quartz, then glanced back at the bat. Its black eyes stared at nothing, glazed. Its mouth hung open a little, its tiny white teeth sharp as rosepricks. Aeriel could see the slight, swift rise and fall of its fragile side as it breathed.

The darkangel shrugged. "I am done with it," he said. "It no longer amuses me."

He brushed it off the wall and over the precipice with one brief motion. Aeriel closed her eyes and turned away. A long moment passed before she could speak.

"Why?" she said, not looking at him. "Why do you torment them?"

"For sport," he answered readily. "I am bored. This castle bores me. My wives bore me. I must have some amusement."

Aeriel opened her eyes. "Need you have killed it?" She was still unable to face him.

The icarus shrugged again; she could hear the rustle of his dozen wings. "Why not?" he said. "There are others."

"Must you catch them at all?" asked Aeriel. "It is so cruel."

"Oh, lizards are even better sport than bats," the vampyre replied. "One can bait them with moon-moths, then pick out their eyes, or tear out their tongues...."

If he continued, Aeriel did not hear; she covered her ears with her hands. Even then she could hear the darkangel laugh at her.

"You are even more sport to bait than the lizards," he said when she took her hands from her ears again.

"There are pleasanter forms of amusement than the tormenting of helpless creatures," cried Aeriel.

"Are there?" said the vampyre. Aeriel felt her skin shrink as he stepped closer, eyed her. "What do you do to amuse yourself?"

Aeriel turned quickly from him, gazed out across the garden. "When I was young," she said, "when I lived in my village in the foothills at the edge of Avaric's white plain, Bomba would tell us tales...."

"Bomba?" said the icarus, drawing back a trace. "Bomba?" He pronounced the name as though he found it absurd. "Who is this Bomba?"

"My nurse," said Aeriel. "No, Eoduin's nurse really...." Her throat tightened and her heart turned at the thought of Eoduin. Even in the company of the wraiths Aeriel had not thought of Eoduin now in months. She found it impossible to think of the wraiths as women, could not imagine any of them had ever been a living maid, as Eoduin had been—but the vampyre was speaking.

"You shall tell me a tale," he said.

Aeriel looked at him. "Now?" she asked.

"Yes, now," he said impatiently. His eyes bored into her like a hawk's. Aeriel swallowed and cast about her for a tale. "Well?" the icarus inquired.

"I shall tell you the tale of the Maiden-Eater," she told him, and began. The tale was a long one, about a kingdom besieged by a dragon and the king's daughter who slew it and the young hero who helped her. The vampyre laughed outright when she came to describing the wyrm.

"Big as a cottage?" he cried at last. "With wings? It is evident that you have never seen a firedrake. They are twenty and thirty times so large, and they certainly cannot fly, though they swim. Incidentally, they do not spit brimstone; they breathe sulfur and flame." The icarus folded his arms and leaned back, looking down on her, his lips curled in contempt. "No mere mortal could have killed one single-handed."

"Her sword *was* magic," said Aeriel.

"The dragon would have killed them both long before she could have used it."

Aeriel looked at the ground. "You have seen dragons, my lord."

"Oh yes. My mother keeps a pair as pets."

Aeriel looked at him. "Your mother?" she said. The word sounded strange from his tongue.

His lips twisted again into a smile. "I do have a mother," he said. "How did you suppose I came to be?" His tone was amused and had no kindness to it. Aeriel dropped her eyes and mumbled something. The icarus pursed his lips a moment, and his look grew farther away. "She is very beautiful, my mother."

Aeriel let another moment go by before she spoke. "What is her name?" she ventured at last.

"And how would I know that?" replied the vampyre, affronted. "Great personages such as she do not hand out their names so freely."

"But you are her son," insisted Aeriel, softly.

The vampyre looked suddenly away, and for the first time his cool assurance flagged. "She will tell me...," he began. "She has promised to tell me—when I come of age."

"And is she...like you?" asked Aeriel, wondering what sort of being mothered vampyres. His hesitation had surprised her.

"You mean a wingèd icarus?" he asked, regaining himself, and flexing his coal-dark feathers. They rustled like fine, stiff silk. "No, she prefers water to air. She is a lorelei."

"And she keeps dragons."

"Yes." A moment's silence followed as the darkangel settled his wings. When next he spoke, it was with no trace of his former faltering. "But hers do not eat maidens. They eat ships." He laughed again, that same cruel and careless laugh. "Ah, me, that was a silly tale you told, but amusing enough. Tell me another."

His tone had taken on a keen edge at the last. "My lord," Aeriel stammered, "I am hungry and tired. I have just spent many hours spinning and weaving for...for your wives"—she had to catch herself lest she, in his presence, say "the wraiths"—"and I..."

He held up his hand, suddenly tolerant again.

"Ah, yes. I sometimes forget you mortal creatures need inordinate amounts of food and sleep. *I* need only a little and a little." He gave her a dismissive nod. "Very well, go have your food and rest, and then come to me in the audience hall, where you shall tell me more of these tales."

FIVE

Prince Irrylath

～

SO AERIEL TOLD THE DARKANGEL TALES, and fed his gargoyles, and spun and wove for his wives, and fished with the duarough in the quiet cave pools, and the day-months passed. She told him all the tales she could remember ever hearing from Bomba, or Eoduin, or anyone else she had ever known. The vampyre seemed to listen with only half an ear, remarking now and again on some improbability in the tale, but he did listen, and Aeriel found no more broken bats or maimed lizards in the garden.

But she found herself now at the last (as she began work on the last of the wraiths' garments) running short of tales, so she asked the duarough for tales, and he told her those he could remember from his nursery days in the caves of Aiderlan, a dozen thousand day-months past. And she told these to the vampyre in the deserted reception hall of the castle, and he listened seemingly with no more attention than before.

Then came the day she told him the tale of the chieftain's son who had lived in a great palace called Tour-of-Kings. It was a tale Dirna had told her, for Dirna had been of the plains folk before she was taken for a slave—told Aeriel the tale while combing out her fine, yellow-tinged hair. It was late, late afternoon, almost dusk in the vampyre's castle. The white sunlight streamed like water over the black slate floor. Aeriel sat on the floor in the warmth of the sunlight, while the icarus stood by the window and picked a flower to pieces as she spoke.

Aeriel said, "This is a tale that Dirna once told me, and it is the last tale that I know. She told it to me one fortnight when we were quite alone, to frighten me, and I do not know if it is true. This is the tale: there was once a woman who was handmaiden to a great chieftain of the plains. And this woman, Dirna, had a child of a day-month old when the chieftain's queen bore him a son. But the queen fell ill, and so Dirna's child was taken from her that she might nurse the chieftain's son.

"But Dirna mourned the loss of her child and

grew to hate the child she nursed. Although she was but a serving-woman, she vowed vengeance against the chieftain, and bided her time. Now it became clear in a few seasons that the fever that had befallen the queen at the birth of her child had left her barren. So when the child had reached his fifth year of age, the queen and her train undertook a pilgrimage across the desert to consult the priestesses of Lonwury about her barrenness.

"So the pilgrimage was made to the shrines of Lonwury across the dry desert, and the queen remained in the sacred city for a year, and her son with her. When all the prayers and the rituals and anointings were completed, the queen gathered her train and started back across the desert. They had journeyed about three-quarters of their way over the waste of dunes when a great wind sprang up that raised the sand in clouds so thick they hid the stars.

"The caravan made camp at once to wait out the storm, but it blew all day-month and on into the shade of night. At last their water ran so low they had to break camp and try to reach the next oasis. The wind drove them then, and they wandered far off their course, till it was day again and the storm abated. They found themselves in a rocky place at desert's edge, amid a maze of canyons, on the shores of a great shallow lake.

"But something was amiss; the queen saw this at once, for nothing grew along the banks of this mere, or in it. A lonely howling, as of jackals, could be heard faintly from the canyons, though not a living creature was to be seen. And when the desert wind blew, not a ripple marred the dark water's surface: it lay still as a mirror, and barren. Those camels that had been allowed to drink sickened and died. The queen ordered at once that no waterskins be filled at this waterhole, and no one was to drink. They would move on.

"They wandered many hours in the gorges and the canyons—and found themselves at the lake again. A second time they went into the rocks, and, after much meandering, found themselves emerging on the lake. Once more they entered the maze, and when this time they again emerged onto the mere, there were mutterings among the people, and talk of witchcraft.

"Camp was made and council held to determine what was to be done. Truly, it seemed the gods were displeased. The queen's priests began to cast the oracle bones to divine the cause. It was a lengthy process and lasted many hours—for the lots were confounded and there was no magic in the counters. The water was all gone by now, the animals dying, but no one dared drink the water of the wide, still lake.

"No one drank, that is, but Dirna. Her thirst became so great that at last it overcame her fear and she crept down to the water in the dark of the night. And while in the distance the unseen jackals sang, she lay down on the sandy bank and cupped her hands to the water. It was cold, colder than shadow, but she drank—drank a handful and was just reaching for another when she saw something in the water.

"It was a small creature, no bigger than a hen, with smooth, translucent skin that seemed purple in the starlight. At first she thought it must be a huge salamander, or a toad. But then it spoke to her in a deep, gravel voice and said, 'What are you doing, trespassing on my mistress's land?'

"'What are you,' cried Dirna, 'and what do you want?'

"'I am a mudlick,' said the hideous creature, 'and I want to know why you are trespassing here.'

"'I was thirsty,' Dirna said. 'We are lost.'

"'We?' the mudlick said. 'Are there more of you?'

" 'Yes,' Dirna told him. 'There is the queen's whole train. Have you not seen them?'

" 'No,' said the mudlick. 'I can see only those things that drink the water. You have drunk, and thus can see me. You told me you came to slake your thirst. What of the others?'

" 'We wish to leave.'

" 'That is not possible,' said the mudlick. 'You have chosen to trespass here, so here you must remain.'

" 'We did not choose. A windstorm drove us here.'

" 'That was not my doing.'

" 'But you must let us go,' said Dirna. 'You must.'

" 'That I will not,' said the mudlick, and turned as if to swim away.

" 'But we will die,' cried Dirna.

" 'I expect you will,' replied the mudlick.

" 'Our water is all gone.'

" 'I do not care.' And with that the mudlick began to depart.

" 'Oh, please,' Dirna besought him. 'I shall do anything you ask, only let us escape.'

" 'No, there is nothing any of you could do for me. I do not need anything from you.'

" 'Don't go; don't go,' Dirna exclaimed. 'Is

there nothing to be done to make you save us?'

"The mudlick wagged his head and started to dive under the dark, glassy surface, when abruptly he stopped. He folded his hands across his slimy chest and trod water for a moment, as if listening to the far-off jackal's song. Then he turned around.

" 'There is one thing, perhaps,' he said.

" 'What is it?' begged Dirna. 'Tell me.'

" 'Well,' said the mudlick, 'my mistress is fond of young boys. Have you any in your train?'

" 'One,' said Dirna. 'There is one.'

" 'How old is he?' inquired the mudlick.

" 'He is six,' the nurse replied.

" 'Hm,' mused the mudlick. 'She likes them younger—babes in arms if possible—but I suppose he will do. Who has charge of him?'

" 'I.'

" 'Very well, bring him down to the water and drown him. Then I shall let you go.'

"Dirna drew back from the creature a little. 'His mother will never consent. She is the queen.'

"The mudlick shrugged. 'As you please,' he said. 'I only thought to do you a kindness. I suppose he really is too old for my mistress's liking....'

" 'I shall do it in secret,' Dirna said. 'I shall tell

her the thirst fever took him and he went to the lake and fell in.'

" 'Tell her the water witch took him,' said the mudlick. 'Then she will think you have the fever, too, and no one will blame you.'

"Then the mudlick swam off and Dirna returned to camp. She slipped into the prince's tent where the boy lay sleeping. There she roused him from his cushions and told him to come out to the lake, that there was something great and wonderful to see, but they must make no noise, so as not to wake the others. The young prince went with her willingly enough, for though she had never been very kind to him, she had never given him reason to distrust her. So, while the distant jackals cried and keened, the two stole out of camp and down to the lake where the mudlick waited.

" 'See?' said Dirna, pointing. 'There it is.'

" 'There is what?' said the prince. 'I see nothing.'

" 'Lean closer,' Dirna urged him. 'Now do you see?'

" 'No,' said the prince. 'What must I look for?'

" 'You must lean closer still, then,' Dirna told him. 'You will know it when you see it.'

" 'But I see nothing,' said the prince, leaning so far forward his face almost touched the water.

" 'Closer,' said Dirna, and this time when he leaned craning to see what she was pointing at, the nurse shoved him hard, so that he fell from the bank and into the lake without so much as a cry. The jackals called. Dirna stood watching to see if he would come to the surface, but the water closed over him with hardly a ripple.

"Then Dirna ran back to camp as quickly as she could and burst into the queen's tent staring wildly and clutching her throat as though she could not breathe. They were a long time getting any sound from her, and for a while that was only shrieks and wails, but finally between much tearing of the hair and tearing her cheeks with her nails, she began to babble and rave.

"And half the time she told them the prince had slipped at the lake's edge and the other half she swore a water witch had caught him by the hair and pulled him in. Finally, she fell into a faint at the queen's feet and could not be roused.

"Whether the queen believed one or the other of the tales, I do not know, but most of the people believed the one of the witch. Many said that the witch had claimed her tribute and would let them go now. Camp was hurriedly struck and the camels loaded for travel. But the queen saw none of this, for she had gone to the lakeshore to weep for her son.

"Then when she returned and saw the caravan ready awaiting, she said, 'Let us depart; this is an evil place.'

"And this time they found their way out of the canyons, and into the desert once more. They soon came upon clear water, and eventually found their way home. Great was the grief of the king when he found his son was dead. The pilgrimage proved fruitless, for the queen was still barren, and at last her husband was obliged to put her aside, and she removed across the Sea-of-Dust to Esternesse.

"The chieftain twice remarried, young daughters of neighboring rulers, but both died very soon, and neither conceived. Blight came to the land, killing the cattle and crops. People began to say the house of the king was accursed, and drifted away. The king grew old before his time, and at last died without heir in a plague year that struck down most of the remaining people.

"Those who were left fled. There was no one to succeed the king, and no one left to rule over. The servants took what goods they might from the palace and departed. The palace guard rounded up those who were left to sell for slaves. Dirna was one of these. She had begun to go blind. Ever since she had drunk the chill waters of that still, dark lake, her sight had worsened, until now both eyes were covered with a white film and she saw nothing anymore of the things of this world.

"She was sold to the satrap of the steeps of Terrain, who gave her along with others who could weave and spin as a gift to his half-sister when she wed the syndic of my village. It is from Dirna that I got this tale. I think perhaps she told it just to frighten me. I do not know if it is true."

AERIEL FELL SILENT AND SAT IN THE SUN on the black slate floor, waiting for some word from the vampyre, but no word came. She looked up and saw him staring off across the room, a slight frown marring the unearthly handsome features of his face.

"Did you not like the story, my lord?" she asked at last.

No expression came into his blank eyes, but his frown deepened a little. "When did this story take place?" he said. His voice was oddly strained.

"Years ago," said Aeriel. "Before I was born."

"And where was the kingdom that the chieftain ruled?" the icarus asked.

"Far away from my tiny village. Far over the white plain of Avaric."

"In what quarter?" the darkangel demanded, his voice so tight Aeriel was startled.

"In the west," she answered. "In the north and west, I think."

The vampyre began to pace suddenly, round and about before the window. His shadow glided back and forth over Aeriel as she sat in the light of the setting Solstar.

"What was the name, the name of this chieftain?" said the icarus, pacing and not looking at her. His one hand was a fist, while the other gripped and wrung his wrist, as though trying, but vainly, to work some shackle free.

Aeriel hesitated. "I do not know," she said. "I cannot remember."

"Then you do not remember the tale very well, do you?" the darkangel snapped.

"Forgive me, lord," said Aeriel. "I tell the tale as best I can."

"The queen," cried the vampyre. "What was the name of the queen?"

Aeriel had to think a moment, long. "Syllva," she said finally. "I think it was Syllva."

"No," said the icarus, his voice suddenly harsh and loud. "You are not remembering it rightly. It was...something else. It was not Syllva."

Aeriel said nothing. The vampyre's voice had fallen to a mutter at the last. He whirled on her abruptly, toying with his necklace now as if it encircled him too tightly, and his shadow hid the light.

"Why are you sitting there so silent?" he cried with sudden suspicion. "Answer me. Say it was not Syllva."

"As my lord commands," said Aeriel, so softly she was afraid he had not heard; the dull clinking of the leaden vials seemed louder. She held her breath.

But the darkangel nodded and half-turned away. He dropped his hand from his throat and leaned against the windowsill. "The boy," he said. "Tell me the prince's name."

Aeriel was at once afraid to answer him and afraid to remain silent. She said, "I cannot remember," and her whisper trembled.

But the icarus seemed hardly to hear. He was staring down the length of the chamber's windowed wall. Aeriel stood up.

"You say his nurse pushed him in?" the vampyre said.

Aeriel nodded, doubting that he saw.

"And his mother went down to the bank and wept for him?"

"Wept tears of blood," said Aeriel.

The icarus said nothing, and his frown was very deep and dark. His anger was pain to her.

"Irrylath," said Aeriel. "I remember now; the prince's name was Irrylath."

The vampyre shuddered and shook his head. "You are mistaken," he told her. There was terrible quietness to his voice.

Beyond him, through the window, Solstar shone in white glory. Already half-hidden by the mountains, in another hour it would be gone. Dark fortnight would descend, leaving only pale stars and waxing Oceanus for light. Aeriel stood waiting.

"Leave me," the darkangel said, not looking at her. The stillness of his voice frightened her. "Do not come again."

Aeriel said nothing—she did not know what to say—and left him.

The Riddling Rime

"YOU MUST KILL THE VAMPYRE," SAID THE
wraiths, one of them, one who could still stand.
She paced back and forth along the wall near
where Aeriel sat on a low stool, spinning. The
golden spindle flashed deep yellow in the white
lamplight. There were no garments left to make.
She merely spun to pass the time.

"What do you mean?" said Aeriel spinning,
spinning a fine golden thread.

Though her duties to them were done, she
would sit with the wraiths for hours on end now,
talking to them, encouraging them to remember
themselves and their pasts, or humming a quiet
tune to herself. Whenever she sang, the wraiths
grew still to listen. But they were pacing now,
those that could stand, or rocking, or writhing, or
uttering little moans.

"What makes you think I could kill the vampyre?" she asked presently, looking down at her hands. Her words were very soft. "I have already tried and failed."

"You looked into his eyes," said one of the wraiths.

"A grave mistake," said another.

"Now he has you in thrall."

"I cannot kill him," said Aeriel.

"But he is evil!" cried the wraiths, and the others echoed: "Evil, evil."

Aeriel stopped spinning and laid the spindle in her lap. She felt her heart grow troubled. "I know," she said. "I know that he is evil, but his beauty unmakes me. Every time he looks at me, I die."

"So each of us thought," said one of the wraiths. "And he has killed us and stolen our souls, so we cannot die."

"I am powerless against him," said Aeriel.

"If we had our souls back, we could depart to deep heaven," said one of them.

Aeriel shook her head frowning. "Your souls are gone. I cannot help you." She took up the spindle again, but the thread broke at once and the golden spool fell to the floor with a bright clink.

"He keeps our souls in little vials," said one of the wraiths, creeping closer across the floor. "You have seen them, the little lead vials on the necklace he wears."

"I thought," said Aeriel, now puzzled, "that vampyres drank souls."

"They do; they do," the wraiths said eagerly, "but he is not a true vampyre."

"Yet," the wraith beside the first one said, and the other nodded.

"Fourteen vials on his leaden chain," said another wraith, the standing one. She bent low over Aeriel as the girl sat on her stool. "Fourteen vials and twelve-and-one filled—with souls. With our souls."

"But," said Aeriel, "if he does not drink them, why does he keep them?"

"He is keeping them for the water witch," said the first, and the others chorused:

"For the witch, the witch."

"For a toast to the witch," shrieked another above the rest. She then fell to the floor writhing and tearing her hair. The other wraiths tried to comfort her, but there was little they could do, for comfort comes from the reaching out of one heart to another, and they had no hearts.

"Who is the water witch?" said Aeriel, bending over the distraught wraith.

"His mother," said the wraith who stood.

"His lover," another said.

"She lives across the desert," said another still, "far and a long way away."

"In a lake," said the fourth, or perhaps it was the first. Aeriel listened now without looking at them—it was impossible to tell which one was speaking; their faces and their voices were all the same.

"They call it the Mirror, or the Dead Lake, sometimes. She has seven sons and they all are vampyres, except this youngest, who will be, very soon. She has sent them all out into the world to prey upon the kingdoms."

"But this one is not quite a vampyre yet," the same, hollow voice from a different quarter continued. "She has not yet taught him all her evils. And he still has his own soul. Nor has he tasted another's yet."

"He has drunk our blood, but not our souls. He is keeping them in the vials the witch has given him. When all twice-seven of them are full, he will return to the Dead Lake and give them to the witch as tribute."

"Then she will drink up our souls and we shall perish—perish truly. Our souls will not ascend as others' do. They will sink into the witch's dark and be *nothing*." Silence a moment. "Though the death of our souls would end our torment, it would be the lorelei's triumph. Even we cannot long for that, Aeriel."

Aeriel looked up at the sound of her name. She had told it to them, but they had never used it. She thought they had forgotten it—as they seemed to forget a dozen other things she told them. She had thought they could remember nothing long.

"You know my name," she said, and the wraiths nodded.

The one who stood before her pulled her features into a grotesque sort of grimace, more like a skull's grinning than a human smile. "We whisper it to ourselves sometimes when you are gone," she said. " 'Aeriel,' we say, 'Aeriel will help us.' "

A sister wraith leaned past her to gaze at Aeriel. "Before you came, little one, we wanted only to forget: our pasts, our present suffering, our fate."

"But you, you brought us back to ourselves a little," another one said; "lightened our despair. Some of us can even bear the remembering now, in tiny snatches."

"A few of us," one wraith said softly, "can even remember our names."

Aeriel's hand went to her throat. She felt as if she were strangling. "Eoduin," she whispered, scanning their withered, wasted faces. "Which one of you is Eoduin?"

The wraiths drew back, shifted uneasily, eyed each other with their hollows. "We shall not tell you," one began.

"Why?" demanded Aeriel. Anger throttled her.

"...unless you help us." Her sister wraiths hissed and nodded their agreement.

Aeriel dropped her hand from her throat, sat a long moment gazing at the wraiths. "What would you have me do?" she said lowly.

"Steal back our souls for us," they cried. "Return to us our souls."

"How can I?" exclaimed Aeriel. "How should I get the necklace from him?"

"You must kill him," said the wraiths.

"I have told you, I cannot."

"You must," said the wraith who stood by her. "Aeriel, you must. How long have you been here?"

"A sixmonth," said Aeriel, feeling a vague dread creep upon her.

"Then in another sixmonth," said the wraith,

"he will bring home a bride. Can you bear it? Can you bear to hear her screams? And we shall scream with her, and the gargoyles. He will make you weave her bridal gown...."

"Her shroud," broke in another.

The first continued, "And attire her...."

"Stop!" cried Aeriel.

"It drove the other one mad," said the wraith. "She had only been here for a year—as you will have been when the time comes. She spun the thread for the bridal gown all day-month before the darkangel flew."

"And he paced restlessly through all the rooms of the castle," another one said. "He came to us and cried, 'All my wives; why are all my wives so ugly? I must have a new one. Spin, girl; spin!'"

"She spun it," continued another one, "but it was of pure horror—so sharp it cut her fingers as she spun—a thread of white terror, and blood."

"And at noon, when the thread was spun," returned the first, "the icarus flew and then the girl wove a long scarf, a sari for the bride, while the sun descended slowly through the star-littered sky—until Solstar was nearly down, and the cloth done, and the vampyre come again with his bride...."

"That would have been Eoduin," cried Aeriel,

standing. Pain and frustration tore at her. "Please," she implored them, "tell me which one."

The wraiths looked at each other, and then at her. They shook their hands. "Help us," they said, "and you will know."

Aeriel stood stupidly, not knowing what to do.

"The girl spun the thread," another wraith continued, "your predecessor." Aeriel shook her head to clear it. "She wove the thread," the withered woman told her, "and the darkangel returned with his bride. The girl washed her and attired her as she was bidden, then brought her to the vampyre's chamber, as she was bidden."

"By then Solstar was down," a wraith that sat at Aeriel's feet said. "The land lay dark, the gargoyles beginning to howl. And the little tiring maid ran all over the castle, trying to find some room where the sound could not be heard, and when she could not, she ran down into the caves and stumbled deep into their darkness before the screaming stopped and she found peace."

"The duarough searched for her long," the wraith beside her said.

"He told us so," her companion murmured.

"Searched for her long and finally found her, convinced her to eat a small something, but she was afraid of the light, and it took him nearly till sunrise to persuade her to come out of the dark into the air of the garden."

"But no sooner had they gone twenty paces," another broke in, "before the sun was up, and the duarough bedazzled. And the girl saw the steps she had strayed to so often, and this time she took them, for the duarough could not call her back."

"Stop," said Aeriel, "stop."

"You know the ending of the tale."

"Yes," gasped Aeriel, "yes."

"Then you must kill him," said the wraiths, "before others die of him."

"I can't," said Aeriel, weeping—for herself, for Eoduin. "He is too beautiful."

"Now," said the wraiths, "while his soul is still his."

"How can such poison be so fair?" cried Aeriel. "How can he be both beautiful *and* evil?"

"He is beautiful," said a wraith, "because there is still some little good in him."

"Good in him?" echoed Aeriel. Could that be? The words put a sudden, irrational hope in her.

"Only a very little," said one of the wraiths. "Not enough to matter."

"He has been taught not to heed it," said her fellow beside her.

"He is evil," insisted another. "He is still woefully evil."

"But there is yet some good in him?" Aeriel cried.

The wraiths muttered among themselves, nodded reluctantly. "His soul is still his," said one. "The witch has drunk his blood, but not his soul."

"But she will," said another, "when she has drunk our souls, then she will drink his. We shall die, die utterly, but he will live on after a fashion, for she has left him his heart."

"It is lead, not flesh," her sister interjected.

"There will be no good left in him then," the one who had spoken formerly continued, "and he will grow ugly. As ugly as we are...."

"No, uglier."

Aeriel sank down on the stool again. She could not speak. A wraith on the floor beside her touched her arm. "As now he drinks blood trying to replenish his bloodlessness, then he will drink souls, in effort to fill up his soullessness—in vain!"

"He will become a drinker of souls, and a true vampyre."

Aeriel put one hand to her mouth; she felt stifled. "The water witch will do this to him," she choked, "drink up his soul and make him ugly?"

Her throat was tight and sore. Pity and anger rose again in her suddenly. "No. I cannot let her have him."

"Then you must kill him," said the wraiths.

"No, I...I must think on it," she finished lamely.

The wraiths gazed at her, hopelessness deepening the hollows of their eyes.

"Perhaps—perhaps there is a way to overcome him without his death...," stammered Aeriel.

"It cannot be done," the wraiths replied.

"I must try."

"He will kill you," they all cried, miserable.

"Then I shall die," she answered, voice trembling; she trembled.

The wraiths turned away from her and started to moan. "Aeriel, Aeriel will not help us!"

Aeriel sat down on the stool again and said nothing more for a time. She unwound the spindle and looped the thread around her elbow into a skein. The skeining took a long while, for the thread was so fine that many yards could be wound onto that tiny spindle, and all the while the wraiths keened and wrung their hands in despair. Aeriel took the skein from her arm, twisted it, and tossed it into the basket, half-full already of the golden skeins.

"I must go down and talk to the duarough," she said, rising from her stool. The wraiths shrieked and wept in defeat. Aeriel left them.

"THE WRAITHS SAY I MUST KILL THE VAMpyre," said Aeriel as she waded carefully across the lighted stream to the far bank where the duarough sat fishing a quiet back eddy with a hook of thorn, a horsehair line, and a rod of cane. Aeriel sat down on the bank beside him.

"What's that you say?" he asked sleepily, head nodding in the fragrant white smoke of the little fire beside him. "Ah well, I thought they would come to it."

Aeriel looked at him, puzzled, and he roused himself enough to notice.

"Oh, yes, they asked all the others, too, you know: the one before you and the one before her. Yes, they asked them all, and all refused—no, I retract that. One of them actually attempted it. She failed, of course." He shook his head. "The others? One of them took her own life rather than face it; another missed her step on the tower stairs and plunged to her death. Another died for loneliness. The last lost her mind and tried to run away." The duarough glanced at Aeriel. "Ah, that castle above is only death and death. Don't spend too much time up there, child. Come down to the caves. Here is life."

At that moment, Aeriel saw a nibble on his line, and the little man fell silent to concentrate on hooking a tiny cavefish barely as long as the hand is broad, and quicker than quicksilver. Aeriel watched him in silence until the fish was caught and strung on the fishline, and the duarough sat baiting his hook again with a white cave cricket.

"I do not want to kill the vampyre," she said at last. "I want ... I want to save the wraiths, but not ... not to kill him."

The duarough glanced at her with upraised eyebrows, then back at his rush pole quickly.

"And how would you propose to do that?" he asked slowly, as if not greatly interested.

Aeriel gazed off across the lighted water and sighed, but she could see out of the corner of her eye that the duarough was watching her intently as she spoke.

"I do not know," she said, "but there must be a way." Her voice did not tense or rise with frustration now. She spoke softly and with conviction. "I am determined to find it."

The duarough eyed her for a long moment then. She did not turn to him, but continued to gaze off across the water. Then he, too, turned back to look out over the lighted stream. He shook his head a trace. "Ah, daughter," he said, "it is a strange thing you would do. Perhaps it is possible; perhaps it is not. But granting for the moment that I might brew a draught that would render the icarus insensible..."

Aeriel turned to him, startled. "You can do that—make such a dram?" She said, "But how?"

He smiled a little then. "I am a son of earth, child. I know a little magic."

"But if you knew how this was to be done," she cried; it was the first time she had ever found herself angry with the duarough, "how is it you have not done it before?"

The little man shook his head again. "I did not say that I could do it," Talb answered gently. "I said that I *might*—with your aid. I could only do the half of it. Another must do the rest."

"But there were others before me," insisted Aeriel, still angry and refusing to soften.

The duarough sighed a trace, very sadly. Aeriel saw a crayfish take his bait without being caught. "But think, daughter; think," her companion said. "What good could lie in such a scheme? He'd only steal the souls of fourteen other maidens to refill his vials."

Aeriel looked away; her anger had faded. "But," she murmured, "if he could be prevented..."

"How, child?" the little man inquired, as solemn as Aeriel had ever seen him. She watched him gather in his line. "Do you propose to chain him, like the gargoyles?"

"No!" cried Aeriel. Her own vehemence surprised her.

The duarough laid his pole on the sandy bank beside him. "Tell me," he said quietly, "why you do not wish the vampyre to perish."

Aeriel drew up her knees and clasped them, stared off toward the wall of the opposite strand. She felt suddenly very cold. "I love his power and his beauty, the magnificence and majesty of him, his splendor and his authority, his surety...." Her voice trailed away.

The little man rose, a bit stiffly, from his sitting place on the bank and looked down at her thoughtfully. "But do you love *him*, child?" the duarough asked.

Aeriel fell silent. "No. I cannot. He has murdered—worse than murdered—my friend Eoduin and twelve other maidens. No. I do not love him." She closed her eyes, defeated. "The wraiths are right. I know that he must die."

The duarough drew in his breath, and let it out again, then nodded, as to himself. He stooped and drew his laden fishline out of the water and stood twirling it slowly, looking at nothing and frowning fiercely as in thought. "Well enough, then," he murmured, as if reluctant; "well enough. He must be stopped, that is decided, and if not one way, then another. Now, first task is to fetch the chalice-hoof of the immortal horse.... The blade, I think, I can attend to myself, and as for the apparatus..."

He muttered other things for a few moments then, things utterly incomprehensible to Aeriel. At first she thought to speak, but then let it go. Sitting there, beside the quiet eddy, in the dimness away from the bright gleam of the fire—though the water had a faint radiance of its own, enough to see by—Aeriel felt suddenly sleepy.

The duarough seemed to come to himself presently; he shook his head a trace as if to clear it and knelt on the bank beside Aeriel, began to fumble about in the many hidden pockets of his robe. He drew out a scaling knife and began to scale his catch.

"I will tell you a rime, child," he said, "one I found in a musty old book lying under dust in the archives. It is a prophecy—not a prediction of what *will* be, mind you," he told her; "no such things exist. But rather a foretelling of what *may* be: a formula for the undoing of the icarus."

Aeriel glanced at him, uneasy, surprised. "I have not said that I will help you," she said, almost beneath her breath. The duarough did not seem to hear. She stared down at her knees, the sand, the water, the opposite shore. Her mind was torn and she knew it should not have been. She should have longed wholeheartedly for the darkangel's destruction, and she did not. "I must think on it," she told the duarough.

Her companion nodded, turning the fish over in his hand and scaling the other side. "Think on it, then, daughter," he said; his tone was kind, "at leisure. But learn the rime also. It is a good thing to know. This is the way of it:

"*On Avaric's white plain,*
　　where the icarus now wings
To steeps of Terrain
　　from tour-of-the-kings,

And damozels twice-seven
　　his brides have all become:
A far cry from heaven
　　and a long road from home—

> *Then strong-hoof of the starhorse*
> > *must hallow him unguessed*
> *If adamant's edge is to plunder*
> > *his breast.*
>
> *Then, only, may the Warhorse*
> > *and Warrior arise*
> *To rally the warhosts, and thunder*
> > *the skies...."*

"There now, do you have that?" the duarough inquired. He had finished his first fish—put it in his sleeve—and started on the second. "That is only the first four couplings, but so much will suffice for now. Can you say it back to me?"

Aeriel made a clumsy attempt and swallowed a yawn; she wondered how long it had been since she had last slept. The duarough gently corrected her wording, recited the poem again and had her say it back. He slipped the second fish into his sleeve as Aeriel tried again. All twelve tiny cavefish had disappeared into the pockets of his robe before Aeriel got the lines recited three times correctly.

"Go now," the little man told her, "and rest. You do not look as though you have seen sleep in a long turn of the stars."

Aeriel rose from the sand. Her limbs felt heavy and her eyelids near shutting.

"Tell me," her companion inquired, just before she waded back across the stream, "do you understand it—the rime, I mean?"

Aeriel shook her head, nodding, sleepy. "What does 'hallow him unguessed' mean?" she asked him.

The little man was winding his horsehair line about his pole. "It means to salute, or to challenge, or to pursue him," he answered, "all unawares."

Aeriel frowned, puzzled. "I thought 'hallow' meant to purify or to bless."

The duarough shrugged his shoulders; his lips smiled slightly. "Words can mean different things, mistress. Perhaps it is I who do not understand the rime." He gave her a rush from the fire for light. "Go now, and rest; the sleep will fix your memory—and we can work more on decipherments when you return."

Aeriel nodded and smiled a little, drowsily. She turned and held her rushlight high as she waded back across the stream.

SEVEN

Darkangel's Dreams

AERIEL AWOKE IN THE DARK OF FIRST nightfall to a sound she had never heard before. It was not the moaning of the wraiths, nor the shrieking of the gargoyles—though they, too, soon added their voices to the uproar. It was rather a kind of shouting, a series of painful cries and then silence again. Or rather, a silencing of the crying voice: the wraiths continued to wail and moan and the gargoyles to chatter and scream as they had not done for many day-months.

Aeriel rose from the mat of rushes where she slept and slipped out into the hall, then down the many steps into the caverns under the castle. As she descended, the cries began again, nearer. Below her, she saw the duarough coming up the bank with a rushlight in one hand.

"What is it?" she cried as she left the last step and her foot touched sandy shore.

Talb came closer to her along the bank. "It is the vampyre, daughter," he said.

"What is wrong with him?" insisted Aeriel. "Is he in pain?"

"Great anguish," the duarough replied, "but not pain. Your tales and stories have given him dreams."

"Dreams?" exclaimed Aeriel. "But he does not sleep...."

"True, true," said the duarough, "he sleeps but yearly, on his wedding night: but that is oblivion, devoid of dreams—a dead and dreamless sleep. No, daughter, these are waking dreams."

Aeriel felt cold and rubbed her arms. "He cries out," she said, "as though afraid. But what is there to fear in dreams?"

The duarough sighed and took the rushlight in his other hand. "Nothing for you and me," he said, "for us who live. But he is mostly dead, and he wishes his mind to be dead to all things but what he himself chooses to think."

Aeriel drew back a bit. "How long will they last?" she asked the other softly.

The duarough shrugged. "They will last as long as they last," he replied, "ceasing for a while and then returning—until they have run their course."

The cries redoubled and Aeriel shuddered. "Is nothing to be done? He suffers so."

"Only sleep can cure these dreams," her companion said. "But he has forsaken sleep."

"If this is my doing," said Aeriel, "I must go to him."

"That you must not," said the duarough, almost sharply.

"Perhaps there is something..."

"There is nothing you may do, daughter."

"I might comfort him."

"He would kill you first," the duarough said. "He is searching the castle for you now; did you know it?"

Aeriel drew back again with a sudden alarm. Not since she had first come to the castle had she feared the darkangel—feared to displease him, perhaps, but not for her life. Gradually she had come almost to disregard his casual threats, for his manner now seemed not at all fearsome to her. Indeed, most times he either treated her with a mocking amusement, or else ignored her altogether.

When first he had brought her to his keep, she had expected death. She had not desired it, but she had been prepared. Now she was not. The wraiths and gargoyles depended on her. The duarough looked to her for company. And the possibility of somehow undoing the vampyre now also lay before her. Her life seemed suddenly less inconsequential, and she found that she did not at all desire to die.

"Come along," the duarough said; "he will be down here shortly. I shall have to hide you."

Aeriel stood unmoving, felt all will and initiative drain from her. The cries were moving closer. "If he calls to me," she said as she realized the truth of it, "I shall go to him."

"Nonsense," said the duarough. "You are only a very little under his power."

Aeriel shook her head. "I shall not want to obey but I shall have to. I cannot resist, his power has grown on me so."

"Then I will stop your ears with wax," said the duarough, coming forward and grasping her hand. "Now come along."

Aeriel went, hardly realizing at first that she did so. "Where are you taking me?" she said in a moment.

"To the treasure room," he answered, pulling her after him. "I had hoped to get you deeper into the caves, but we've no time now. Don't fear; we shall be safe enough in the treasure room, only we must *hurry*."

They splashed across the stream and clambered onto the opposite bank. Aeriel could hear the cries of the vampyre drawing closer, was beginning to be able to distinguish some words. They were disconnected, made no sense, but their effect was hypnotic. She wanted to stop, to listen, to stand forever trying to catch their meaning. The duarough pulled her over to the ivory door and practically had to drag her through.

The door closed behind them and the sound of the words diminished. As they moved out from behind the partition and into the room itself, the noise lessened further. There burned the little fire of driftwood in the middle of the room as before. The duarough led her over to it. She realized dimly that the shouting had now ceased altogether. She sank down beside the fire, feeling suddenly very spent.

"I shall go and fetch the wax now," said the duarough. "I shall be gone for a little while. He will begin calling you again very shortly, no doubt. Do not answer. Do not even listen; hold your ears if you must—and *stay* in this room."

The duarough turned away from her then and

left by the other hidden door. Aeriel lay down and laid her head on her arm. She listened to the soft, irregular snapping of the driftwood as it burned. Then she heard the darkangel again; he was much closer. She knew he must be in the caves. He was calling to her. She shut her ears.

Lying on her side, with her ear so close to the ground, she could hear his footsteps crunching back and forth in the sand. She knew he was pacing along the far riverbank, searching for her. He called again, but the rock and her hands on her ears muffled and changed the sound—she could not tell what he said.

She heard a little splash, as though perhaps one of his feet had slipped partway into the water. She heard him cry out in the same moment and scramble back as if the touch of living water burned. There were no footsteps for a while, and then they tramped off down the bank—irregular now, uneven: he was limping.

Aeriel uncovered her ears and sat up. She glanced about her: the empty room stood still and unchanging—all was quiet. She waited, and presently the duarough returned with a lump of beeswax in one hand and a great musty book in the other. He seated himself by the fire and laid the book to one side. Aeriel glanced at it curiously, but did not ask him what it was. He held the beeswax close to the fire to warm it. Aeriel watched him bend and work it with his hands. The greyish wax was hard, translucent, smelled sourish-sweet. It softened slowly.

The vampyre's shout rang out so close and clear this time that Aeriel jumped. She could tell by the sound of it that he was on the near side of the bank.

"He's returned," she said, shaken. She had not expected him back so soon.

The duarough nodded. "He is afraid to go very far into the caves."

Aeriel looked at him, startled. "Afraid? But he is so strong and sure. I did not think he could be afraid of anything."

The duarough shook his head and worked the wax. "Oh, he is a great coward. He is afraid of the dark and of his own dreams. He only comes down here now and again to search for..."

"Afraid of the dark?" said Aeriel. "But..."

The duarough laughed. "Yes, yes. I know. He is a creature of darkness, but the witch has not yet taught him to love the dark. Ah, but when she takes his dreams from him, he'll no longer fear it. It will be the light, then, that he'll shun."

"The witch?" said Aeriel. "You mean the water witch, his mother?"

The duarough snorted, but said nothing more for a minute. Aeriel looked at him curiously. "She is not his mother," he said at last.

"What do you mean?" said Aeriel.

"The lorelei are barren," the duarough said, "as are their 'sons,' the icari. They have forsaken life—no life can spring from them. What children they call theirs they must steal at an early age...."

The vampyre began to call again. He was some way up the bank by this time, possibly even into the next chamber. Sitting up as she was, with her ears uncovered, Aeriel could hear him perfectly.

"Where are you?" he cried, and the dull echoes repeated the cry. "Answer me!"

His voice sounded ugly to her—angry and on edge. Aeriel shuddered and tried not to listen. She watched the duarough, the fire, glanced around the great, bare room—anything to keep from hearing him. His voice became suddenly smooth, almost sweet.

"Come out," he called, "and I promise not to be angry. You haven't really displeased me, but I must talk to you. Won't you come out?"

His words rang true, sincere. Hearing them, Aeriel could almost believe.

"You know I'm very fond of you," the vampyre said; his voice sounded so pleasant now. "You've nothing to fear from me. Come out."

Aeriel had risen to her feet without realizing it. She had always obeyed him. The compulsion was strong to do so now.

"I won't hurt you," the icarus said.

"He's lying," said the duarough. "He'll kill you."

"Listen to me," the darkangel called; "you shouldn't stay down here in these twisting caves; you'll lose your way. Come out now, or I shall be angry."

The duarough held her eyes with his and would not let them go. Aeriel backed away from him toward the door.

"All I want," cried the icarus, "is for you to promise not to tell me any more of those tales. Then we can be friends again. Agreed? Why won't you answer me?"

The duarough stood up. Aeriel moved for the door. "Daughter," he said, "don't go to him."

"I can't help it," cried Aeriel softly. "I know he is lying, but I cannot disobey him."

"Try. You are only a very little under his power, child—you can still free yourself if only you want to."

Aeriel moaned in despair. "But I do not want to," she faltered. "I want to go to him. I want to spend all my life in his service. I want to die for him."

"Once you wanted to kill him," the duarough said.

Aeriel closed her eyes and whispered, "Yes." That also was true.

"And would you leave the wraiths to their fate of death?" the duarough said.

Aeriel shook her head. "No. No."

"Then you must not let him take you."

"Listen," cried the vampyre, frustration beginning to override the honey in his tone. "You needn't fear about the bats and the lizards. I won't catch them anymore if you don't want...." His voice broke suddenly with rage and he shouted, "Where are you, you worthless little drudge? Come out now so I can kill you. How dare you resist me? Obey!"

Aeriel was shaking. She could not move.

"Why?" the darkangel roared. His voice rose and trembled. "Why have you done this to me? Telling me tales, sending me dreams—lies! They are all of them lies. Tell me no more of them...."

He broke off suddenly. The timbre of his voice changed, grew frantic. He was not speaking to her anymore.

"No, go away. Go away," he said in a frightened whisper. "I don't want to think about you anymore. I left you behind a long time past. Why have you come back? Go away!"

Silence. For a moment Aeriel could hear nothing but the fire snapping and her own uneven breathing.

"What is it?" she breathed.

"His dreams," said the duarough softly.

"Don't come near me!" shrieked the vampyre. "Don't look at me. Don't touch me. I am the master here. You must obey me. Obey me...."

His voice trailed off into a wail. Aeriel was shaking so hard she could scarcely speak.

"I," she said. "I have done this to him."

The duarough shook his head. "He has done this to himself. What you have done, and will do, may be..."

"I want to go to him," said Aeriel.

"Do not," said the duarough sharply. "Even now he is treacherous and dangerous."

"He weeps," said Aeriel.

The duarough shook his head.

"I can hear him," she insisted.

"He has no blood," the duarough said, "nor tears. He is baiting you."

"You are wrong," answered Aeriel. "I think he truly suffers."

"That may be," the duarough told her. "But he will recover."

Aeriel listened to the vampyre's dry sobbing. He moaned.

"Leave me. Let me be. Why do you haunt me so? I want no more dreams, no dreams. Please . . ."

Aeriel put her hands to her ears and sank down. "I cannot stand this anymore. Stop my ears."

The duarough came forward, the beeswax in hand. The wax was hot and soft in her ear. He pressed it into place, then turned her head to reach the other. He pulled off a piece of wax from the lump, but before he could put it in, the icarus called again, from farther away than before. She heard him limping upstream along the bank. His voice shook a little, but that was all. He was trying to sound pleasant.

"Where are you?" he cried. "Come out. There's no need to be afraid. . . ."

Aeriel let the duarough press the warm wax into her ears, and then all was quiet.

How long she might have dozed, Aeriel could not tell. When she awoke, the duarough was taking the wax from her ears. The great book lay open on the sand across from her; its pages were covered with many rows of runes, and the illuminated picture of a great snowy heron. The small white fire flickered as before—it never seemed to burn down, and she had never seen the duarough add kindling to it. When his careful, stubby fingers had gotten most of the warm wax from her ears, she could hear it snapping quietly now and again.

"Is it safe?" she said, sitting up and taking the last bits of beeswax from her ears herself. Her mind was clear now, no longer under the dark-angel's spell. She felt stronger, and more sure.

"Safe enough for the moment, I should think," the duarough replied. "He has gone off upstream into the higher caves. I have closed a few passages and opened others to confuse him. I think he will be lost up there for a while yet. Are you hungry? Here, eat this."

He produced from one of his many hidden pockets a large white mushroom—one of the many that grew in the caves. Aeriel took it gladly. It was fluffy as angelfood, but at the same time very filling. The duarough went back over to the fire and knelt beside his book. Aeriel gazed at the illuminated picture of the heron while she ate, and wondered what it signified.

"I have done some reading while you slept," the duarough said, "and have made something for you. Come and I will show you."

He rose and walked past her then to the door behind the partition. Aeriel followed hesitantly, half-expecting the vampyre to stand concealed just beyond the corner, ready to snatch them the moment they emerged. But no vampyre lurked. As they came through the door and walked down to the water, Aeriel saw moored to a stake driven in the sand a tiny skiff, shallow as a marsh boat, made of something pearly and translucent like horn or shell, with a heron's bust—head dipped, wings outspread—carved as figurehead upon its prow. The craft had a single tiny sail, so light that even the slight cave wind swelled it so the craft bucked and danced in the water like an eager horse.

"She is so beautiful," said Aeriel, drawing toward the little vessel like a moth to light. She knelt and laid her hand upon its slender prow. The skiff bobbed and rubbed her hand exactly like a pony. "What is her name?"

"I have christened her *Wind*," said the duarough, "*Wind-on-the-Water*, in hope that she will bear you as swiftly as her name."

"Bear me?" said Aeriel. "I am not going...."

"But you must, child; don't you see? The icarus will kill you if you stay."

Aeriel shook her head and stroked the little ship sadly. "I cannot leave here. I am in his power, yes, but I have sworn to rescue the wraiths."

"He will not let you," said the duarough. "Believe me; your only hope to save them lies in going now and doing as I say."

Aeriel looked at him a long moment. Half her heart went out to the little vessel, yearned to go skipping away across the water, but the other half still longed after the darkangel, and wished never to leave him.

"You are not just sending me to safety, then."

The duarough shook his head. "No safety lies in this departure, Aeriel."

"You have a task for me to perform."

This time he nodded. "You must sail downriver through all the caves and under the plains till you come to the gorge where the river emerges. This will put you miles from the castle, and far from the eyes of the gargoyles—oh yes, daughter: well fed no less, they'd bite the hand that's fed them—raise the alarum if you left in their sight. When you come to the gorge, you must leave the boat and traverse the plains and the sanded desert."

He paused for a moment, took breath in order to collect himself. His words were hurried. Aeriel listened.

"It will be a long trek," he told her. "I know not how long it will take you—many day-months and many to return. You must walk toward Oceanus, walk over the dunes until the Planet hangs directly above you in the heavens and you stand at the center of the world. There you must seek after the starhorse—he of the strong hoof, undying. Bring back what you may of him, for it is by the hoof of the starhorse that the icarus will fall. Come now, say me the riddle again, that I may know that you have it fast in your mind."

Aeriel recited the rime to him then, and indeed it was as clear in her memory as if she had known it since childhood:

"On Avaric's white plain,
            where the icarus now wings
To steeps of Terrain
            from tour-of-the-kings,

And damozels twice-seven
            his brides have all become:
A far cry from heaven
            and a long road from home—

Then strong-hoof of the starhorse
            must hallow him unguessed
If adamant's edge is to plunder
            his breast.

Then, only, may the Warhorse
            and Warrior arise
To rally the warhosts, and thunder
            the skies."

The little man folded his arms and nodded as he listened.

"Well enough, then. Good, child. Do not forget it." He unfolded his arms. "Now, as I told you, I do not know how long this journey will take you. I shall try to delay the vampyre, and I shall send you a helpmate if I can." He started. "Oh, I almost forgot."

He reached into one of his many hidden pockets and pulled out a little sack of black velvet, drawn together at the top with a drawstring. He handed it to her.

"I have put ample provisions in there for your journey," he said.

Aeriel gazed at the bag in bewilderment. It lay light and limp in her hand. "But it's empty," she said.

The duarough smiled. "Not so. Pull it open and look inside."

Aeriel did so. The interior was black and filled with nothing.

"Now close your eyes and reach inside," the duarough instructed.

Aeriel obeyed. She felt something smooth and round, the size of a fist. She pulled it out. It was a pale golden fruit.

"Reach in again," the duarough told her.

This time Aeriel pulled out an oyster, still damp and cold in its shell. Bidden again by the duarough, she reached in once more and pulled out a handful of almonds. Again—a steamed crayfish wrapped in rushes. Again—a bunch of white grapes. She looked at the duarough. He smiled modestly, blushing a trace.

"Oh yes, my dear, I am a bit of a magician. One can't help but learn a thing or two in—"

A shout interrupted him, and then a crash far upstream, several chambers away. It sounded as though some heavy door had just been thrown aside. Aeriel gasped. The duarough paled.

"By the Pendarlon," he murmured, "he's found the way out already. I am not half the magician I thought I was. Quick, girl, into the boat."

Aeriel had no time to think, or even to say a

word. The duarough was hurrying her into the little craft, which, for all its lightness, hardly dipped when she stepped in and settled herself on the cross-plank behind the mast. She replaced the golden melon and other foodstuffs in the black velvet sack and slipped it onto her sash.

Meanwhile the duarough freed the mooring from the stake and the skiff leapt away from shore like a steed given its head. He scarcely had time to toss in the cord before she was out of reach. Aeriel turned and would have called some farewell, save that the duarough put his finger to his lips and gestured back upstream toward where the vampyre must be, though they heard no more noise.

Aeriel had just raised her hand to wave, when *Wind-on-the-Water* sped through the archway into the next chamber and the little man behind on shore was lost to her sight. Aeriel sat motionless, gazing astern. She felt suddenly abandoned and alone. After a moment, she sighed and dropped her hand, then turned and looked ahead to see where the river led.

EIGHT

Quest and Flight

~

THE JOURNEY WAS LONG AND AT THE SAME
time swift. The river veered first right, then left,
and seemed to be descending in a strange, irregular spiral through the rock on which the
vampyre's castle rested. It ran down, ever down,
through an endless series of natural chambers.
Some were huge and wide, filled with curtains and
columns, and pointed pedestals of crystal lime.
Others were long and low, more tunnels than
chambers.

In one, there was an opening in the wall
through which she could see the stars. In their pale
light and the brighter, warmer glow of the river,
she saw that this was the haven of the bats. They
flew in and out of the opening and through the
cave like silver moths, and many of them clung
to the walls and ceilings, like a mass of withered

leaves. Their twittering, what she could hear of it, was high and wild and airy thin. Aeriel laughed and was surprised to hear how thick and deep her voice sounded next to theirs.

Another chamber, hours later, farther down into the heart of the mountain, was latticed with silver combs dripping honey like liquid amber. The great stingless bees that tended the combs were greyish-gold with bands of rose, and covered with velvet fur. She watched them crawling about their waxworks, building the six-sided chambers, filling them with sweet, thick honey, feeding their pale, formless young. On the far side of the room, on the greatest comb of all, Aeriel beheld the queen—larger than the rest, surrounding by her nurses and clumsy drones.

Then, much farther on, after Aeriel had drifted into sleep, she awoke to find herself in the greatest chamber she had yet seen. It was huge and dark. She could not see the limit before or behind. What she could see was the ceiling above dotted with glowworms, whose pale yellow light burned like phosphor. The air itself was filled with fireflies that hovered in the dark like candle flames. The stream ran nearly flat here, and Aeriel realized it must have emerged from the mountain now and be running under the plains. The cave of the glowworms ran on and on. She fell asleep again and dreamed she was riding through deep heaven, surrounded by the stars.

When next she awoke, the first thing she thought was that she was still in the cave of the glowworms, but then she noticed that the lights overhead were smaller, silver, and Oceanus shone hoary blue in the middle heavens off to the right. There was a narrow beach on either side of her, then low, steep banks. The second thing she noticed was that her little craft was no longer moving. Its sail was full and it still bounced and bobbed in the bright water of the stream, but it had run aground on a little sandy shoal.

She got out of the boat to try to free it, but before she could do so much as lay a hand on it, it bounded away from her, merry as a greyhound. Then Aeriel remembered that she must abandon the little boat anyway, now that she had reached the plain; it was as well it had abandoned her. She checked to see that the small velvet bag was still firmly tied to her belt, then walked across the beach and scrambled up the bank.

At the top of the bank, she looked back at the stream, for a last view of *Wind-on-the-Water,* but she saw no sign of her—only a great heron wing-ing low over the river running. The bird shone very white, whiter than pure snow in the earth-shine. It beat its wings twice, veered right and rose out of the gorge into the nightdark sky. Aeriel watched it sail away over the plain toward Oceanus.

The wind blew over Avaric, bowing the grass and lifting Aeriel's hair. She laughed. She had not realized how much the vampyre's castle had oppressed her until now that she was free of it. Looking back, she saw it only as a tiny point on the far horizon. She said the rime then once more, softly to herself:

> "On Avaric's white plain,
>   where the icarus now wings
> To steeps of Terrain
>   from tour-of-the-kings,
>
> And damozels twice-seven
>   his brides have all become:
> A far cry from heaven
>   and a long road from home—
>
> Then strong-hoof of the starhorse
>   must hallow him unguessed
> If adamant's edge is to plunder
>   his breast.

Then, only, may the Warhorse
and Warrior arise
To rally the warhosts, and thunder
the skies."

Then she turned her face toward Oceanus, and set off across the plain.

THE TRIP PROVED MORE ARDUOUS THAN she had imagined. She walked long hours through the high, grey-green grass, then sank down to rest, her legs trembling. She ate of the foods in the little pouch, and slept on the bare ground—which was light and springy. The wind on the plain was warm, and she did not feel the want of a fire.

Sometimes, far away to the right or left, she saw small birds or wild asses with bands of golden-green streaking their flanks. Also she saw antelope, grasshens, and once two wild hunting dogs of mottled grey and tan. They watched her from a distance and yipped softly, but no more. Gradually, as the fortnight wore on, and all the walks and stops and sleeps blended into one, the stars shifted, and Oceanus, waxing to full and then waning again, rose a little higher in the sky.

As she moved on across the plain, the soil grew

looser and drier; the grass stood shorter and sparser. Eventually, the grass gave way to low scrub, and when at last the sun rose over the western mountains, Aeriel found herself at the edge of the scrubland, and the beginning of the dunes.

She set off at once across the sand, which was white with a pale, orange cast to it. Though utterly dry, it had a faint cohesion—a sort of crust had formed on the surface of the sand. Though this was neither thick nor strong, Aeriel found that if she stepped lightly and carefully, it would not break beneath her weight—but if she stepped hard, or paused a moment in her pace, the surface crumbled, and her feet sank ankle-deep in soft, coarse sand.

She had not been traveling long after sunrise, nor had she gotten very far into the desert, when she heard a shout, far in the distance behind her. She paused, startled. It had been almost a fortnight since she had heard a human voice. She half-turned, puzzled, expectant, almost elated at the thought of meeting someone, anyone—and then the soft crust crumbled beneath her feet. She saw him: the darkangel, coursing toward her out of the north like a greathawk on his wings of utter black.

She had no thought of hiding (for where was there she could hide?) nor of facing him. If she were to save the wraiths, she realized, she must not let him take her. And the whole of the duarough's as-yet-untold plan now rested on her as well. She ran.

Light across the surface of the sand she ran— it held just long enough for her foot to leave its face before caving in, to leave a jagged row of footmarks in the dunes. Over one rise and then the next, she fled, felt her hair streaming out behind her. She did not look behind.

The dunes sped past, for a long time, it seemed—many heartbeats. Her breath was running short, her pulse was racing; her legs were growing tired. Then she gasped as she felt the wind of the darkangel's wings on her back and knew he was in the air above her and just behind. "Turn around," he cried; his words were a deafening snarl. "Turn around and face me!" She did not listen; she did not answer—she ran on.

He swooped. She fell to the sand and rolled. His wing tips brushed her cheek; then he was gone, rising into the air for another pass. Aeriel got to her feet and fled. The sand had broken when she had dived. There was sand in her hair now, in her eyes, in her ears. She batted it from her lips, sucked in her breath, and ran on.

The vampyre swooped again, not deep enough. She ducked and dodged and continued running. The icarus gave a scream of rage and pulled up for another try. His scream was answered—from across the dunes sounded a roar: rolling, thundering. Aeriel spun around. Behind her on the crest of a dune stood a great beast, a lyon with a mane of gold. His body was white-golden; he shone like the sun.

The icarus screamed again in his rage and the lyon challenged him with a roar that shook the air. For a moment she thought they would battle: the darkangel hovered in the black sky just above him; the bright lyon crouched ready to spring. Then suddenly the icarus turned and rushed headlong through the air toward Aeriel. The great lyon sprang in pursuit. Aeriel started like a deer, and fled.

They were both behind her, and very close. She could hear the lyon's paws touching the sand, the vampyre's wings beating the still air. They were closing on her rapidly. Presently she caught sound of their breathing—the darkangel's harsh and hoarse, the lyon's smooth and deep. She realized they would reach her at almost the same instant and had just decided she would surely be torn apart between them, when the vampyre caught her.

First by the hair, then by the arm he hoisted her aloft. His hand was so cold it burned. She looked into his eyes and they were colorless as egg-white, ferocious, full of madness. He bit her throat near the shoulder and Aeriel screamed. The lyon sprang. His collision with the darkangel jolted her, staggered the vampyre in midair. The icarus shrieked and let go of her as the great cat raked his face.

Pressed between the two of them, she could not fall. Her right side froze and trembled against the darkangel's bloodless flesh, while her left side burned and writhed in the heat of the lyon's body. With his other paw, the great cat dragged four long gashes down the vampyre's shoulder. The icarus twisted away. The lyon dropped to earth. Aeriel fell and lay stunned on the sand, looking above her at the deep, bloodless wounds in the darkangel's face and shoulder.

Before the vampyre could recover himself, the lyon had sprung between him and Aeriel. The pale golden cat's huge head bent over her. She shut her eyes and prepared to die. His mouth closed gently, firmly over her arm. Pulling her up, he half-shrugged, half-slung her over his shoulder, then bounded off in great strides across the dunes.

Aeriel lay dazed. Her throat where the icarus had bitten her was an agony of fire and ice. She felt so winded she could hardly breathe. She felt her arm held hard in the lyon's mouth—his great, pointed teeth pressed into her flesh, but they did not so much as break the skin. She felt the rush of wind along her body and the movement of the lyon's lithe, hard muscles beneath the skin as he ran. His coat was soft and warm as sunlight, and she sensed that beneath, his flesh was hotter still. He smelt like heated oil and sandalwood.

She saw the icarus in the sky behind them. He made no attempt to follow, but hovered in the air watching them, screaming in his fury. The rhythm of his churning, raven wings seemed altered somehow—rougher, oddly strained. She could not fathom it. He grew farther away with each bound of the lyon. At last she saw him turn and start a slow, limping flight back southward toward the castle.

Then Aeriel realized she was bleeding from the throat. Blood streamed from the wound the vampyre had made. She felt cold; she shivered. The wind was cooling and drying the blood on her kirtle, made the pale, soaked garment cling to her side. She stared at it, appalled. Presently, she grew very light-headed, and in a little time more, felt herself slipping into a swoon.

WHEN SHE AWOKE, SHE WAS LYING ON the sand. The sun was hot on her face. Her throat ached. There was an intermittent sound of splashing over to her left. She listened to it, not wanting yet to open her eyes. She was just beginning to drift into a dream when a few drops of water sprinkled her cheek. She heard the plash of water again, and in a moment, more drops fell. She blinked and opened her eyes. The lyon sat on the sand beside her, shaking water from one great paw onto her face.

"Ah, you are awake, child," he said. His voice was very quiet and deep. "How do you feel? Can you rise?"

"I don't know," she said. "I feel weak."

The lyon nodded. "That is to be expected. The bite of an icarus is no mean thing. Come, you must try to sit up. Your wound must be attended to."

Aeriel pulled herself upright into a sitting position. For a moment, the sky tilted crazily and threatened to fall. She rested her head on her knees. Only now did she begin to wonder that she was not dead, that the lyon had rescued her from the vampyre, and that he spoke with a human manner and voice.

She rested her head on her knees. She knew that there was water nearby. She reached out her hand and felt wet sand, then liquid. She dipped her hand into the water, brought her cupped palm to her lips and drank a little, but swallowing was painful, difficult. She bathed her neck; the wound burned at the touch of water, but she felt the pain ease.

She drank again. The water was warm and faint blue-green in color. Its taste reminded her vaguely of cress, and it smelled of life. She raised her head from her knees a bit, and saw that she was sitting beside a tiny pool hardly more than a puddle in the sand. A sprinkling of miniature water plants dotted the surface, and among them a handful of tiny frogs, chirping. She saw four snails with spiral shells on the bottom and two at the water's edge.

"There," said the lyon. "Does that help the hurt?"

Aeriel started. He sat so unobtrusively, she almost had forgotten him. "Yes," she said weakly. "Much."

"Strain some of the floating plants out of the

water with your hand and plaster them to the wound," he instructed. "They will help it more than just the water."

Aeriel did so. The little flecks of green were surprisingly pungent and when she pressed them to her neck, their oily coating seeped into the wound with a soothing warmth. Gradually the cold, numbing ache began to abate. Still she felt giddy, at times almost faint, but no more in pain. After a time, she realized she was hungry, and reached without thinking into her pouch for food. She remembered the lyon suddenly and glanced at him.

"Are you hungry?" she inquired timidly. "Would you like something to eat?" Despite his reserved and gentle manner, she still felt a lingering fear of being leapt upon and devoured.

The lyon bowed his head with consummate grace and replied, "I should be honored."

She fumbled in the little bag, rejecting first the rosepear and then the stalk of sweet cane that came to hand. At last she found something suitable, a boiled crayfish. She held it out to him timorously, half-afraid that he would snap it up in his great jaws, and her hand along with it. Instead, he bent his head and took it carefully. Then, reclining, he placed the crustacean between his paws and proceeded to peel it with a delicacy and dignity she could scarce believe. She felt foolish and ill-mannered nibbling on the small globe of cheese she had taken for herself.

"Would you like something else?" she asked quickly, when he had done.

"Thank you, daughter, no," he said graciously. "You must save the rest for yourself."

Aeriel saw now that he had taken her first offering not from hunger, but from courtesy. At least, she was glad to see, he was not ravenous. She nibbled her cheese and felt very worn.

"You saved me from the vampyre," she said at last. "Why?"

"It is my duty to protect all creatures within my borders, child," the great cat replied. "And I am not particularly fond of icari."

"I never saw you before he came," said Aeriel. "Were you nearby all the while?"

"Oh no, daughter, no. I had to come from a great distance to find you."

"To find me?" said Aeriel. Her head was feeling very heavy; she rested it on her hand. "You knew that I was coming?"

The lyon nodded. "A white heron told me you

would be crossing my south border about dawn. I had already been patrolling for some hours before I spotted you."

"A white heron," murmured Aeriel. *"Wind-on-the-Water."*

"Perhaps she was called so once," the lyon said. "But when she came to me, she said her name was *Wing-on-the-Wind."*

Aeriel said nothing. Her eyelids drooped; her stomach lay full in her and slightly queasy. She felt restless and drowsy at once. The sky tilted slowly off to the left.

"Lie back on the sand, child," the lyon was saying. His voice sounded far, a very long way away. "You are fainting."

Aeriel lay back on the sand; the world steadied a little. "I must find the starhorse," she murmured, "the equustel...."

The lyon bent over her again. "Daughter, I know your quest," he said. "The white heron told me. But you have lost much blood to this wound and will be a while yet healing. I will give you into the hands of the desert folk, who will tend you until you are fit to travel again."

Aeriel shook her head and muttered something. She did not want to wait; there was not time. It would not be many months before the vampyre took another bride—his final bride. She must find the starhorse and return with him to the duarough before that.

But she found herself too weak to make protest to the lyon. Her eyes slid shut and she slipped into a doze. Later she half-woke, or perhaps it was a dream: a dream of strange music played on woodwinds and tambours, and of a long train of dark people with banners and walking sticks, and of their leader, a tall woman, conferring with the lyon. Aeriel could not hear what they were saying, though now and again they glanced back at her.

The lyon and the woman parted. Aeriel watched him disappear over the dunes. The dark people came and stood about her. Then, lifting her carefully onto a litter, they quietly bore her away.

NINE

Eclipse

~⁓

THE PEOPLE OF THE MA'A-MBAI WERE tall and dark. They had the darkest skin Aeriel had ever seen, a dusky rose hue the color of cinnamon. They wore loose, sleeveless smocks of pure white seedsilk and carried long, knobbed walking staves. They owned few possessions, spoke softly to each other as wind among reeds, and their hair grew close to the scalp in coarse, tight curls.

They were nomads, Aeriel discovered, combing the desert for game and other foodstuffs. That they had taken away her torn and bloodied kirtle and given her one of their own garments, Aeriel realized the first time she had awakened clear-headed enough to take in her surroundings.

Their leader, Aeriel learned, was called Orroto-to—a tall, spare woman of middle years and few words. She tended Aeriel's wound with poultices and herbal broths. At first Aeriel slept much, but gradually, as Solstar rose toward its zenith and Oceanus waned, she felt her strength beginning to return. And the Ma'a-mbai bore her along with them as they moved east.

At one point, after much travel and little resting, the Ma'a-mbai laid their camp next to a stony wall, drove their staves into the sand, and hung their canopies from them. Aeriel they laid in the shade of one of these, and Orroto-to knelt beside her, feeding her choice bits of a roasted desert hare. Aeriel turned to her; she was feeling well enough for conversation.

"The desert cannot hold much food," said Aeriel.

Orroto-to tore off another tender bit. "There is enough," she said.

Aeriel savored the taste of the morsel in her mouth. "Still," she said, "there would be more for your people if I were not here." She had not touched the duarough's velvet pouch—now worn on a thong about her neck—since she had been with the desert folk. Their hospitality did not permit a guest to draw upon her own provisions.

The desert woman checked the poultices on Aeriel's throat and added a few drops of water from a shallow dish on the sand beside her. "The Pendarlon has asked us to see to you," she said, "and that is enough."

"The Pendarlon?" said Aeriel, puzzled. "Who is that?"

Orroto-to gave a throaty laugh; her wise, pale brown eyes danced. "You do not know? He is the one who rescued you."

Aeriel gazed at her, surprised. "The lyon?" The other nodded. Aeriel glanced down. She had occasionally heard the people of her village exclaim oaths of "By the Pendarlon," but she had never used the expression herself. "But," she said at the last, "what does it mean?"

"Pendar-lon," her physician explained. "It means 'Warden of Pendar.'" That her voice held no rancor encouraged Aeriel to inquire further.

"And where is Pendar?" she asked.

Orroto-to looked at her in surprise. "Why, this," she exclaimed with a nod that took in everything around them. "All that you see about you to the horizon and beyond."

"But I thought," said Aeriel, "I thought that Pendar was a great land of cities and ancient wisdom. Talb said the Old Ones lived in Pendar."

The desert woman nodded sadly, offered Aeriel the last morsel, but Aeriel shook her head. She had eaten enough. "Once, little pale one, once. Their glory is all laid waste now." She fed the tidbit to one of the thin, sandy camp dogs and washed the grease from her dark fingers in the shallow bowl. "The Old Ones are few and far between. They are growing afraid of the outside—most of them hide in their domed cities now, far from each other, shut off from the world." She shook the water from her hands and waved them slowly to dry. "They come out so seldom now that most of your people think they all died years ago." The wisewoman shook her head. "Not so. You should know better."

"What does the Pendarlon do?" inquired Aeriel.

"Ah," said Orroto-to, "he runs back and forth over the land, guarding the borders and looking to the safety of his people."

"Who are his people?" said Aeriel.

The dark chieftess gave another low, throaty laugh and gestured toward the Ma'a-mbai youths filling their waterskins at the well. "We are his people," she said. She looked up at two skyhawks circling lazily in the black heavens. "Those are his people." She nodded toward a dune where three sand-rats scampered and played. "There are his people," she said, "and there." In the distance a herd of gazelle leapt and bounded like tumblers. "Every creature within his borders is one of his people," Orroto-to said.

"He is your ruler, then," said Aeriel, but the dark woman shook her head.

"He does not rule us. No one can rule us. No one can rule anyone who does not first agree to the ruling." She smiled a trace at Aeriel and patted the little camp dog, which was whining for more tidbits. "One must rule oneself."

"But," began Aeriel, puzzled, "but if the Pendarlon..."

"He is our warden and our guide," the chieftess told her, "and everyone is free."

Aeriel shook her head, still not understanding. "But do you, Orroto-to, not rule the Ma'a-mbai?"

"I but lead them," the other replied, "and they follow only so long as they choose."

Aeriel considered it for a long moment, then, and did not understand. "But what am I now?" she asked finally. "Now that I am within the lyon's borders. Have I, too, become one of his people?"

"No," her companion answered, getting up from the sand and shooing the small dog away. "You belong still to the Avarclon, though you are the leosol's guest and under his protection now."

"And who is the Warden of Avaric?" asked

Aeriel. She had never before heard of an Avaric-lon.

"The Starhorse," said the other, straightening. "The equustel."

"The equustel," cried Aeriel, sitting up suddenly. "But I am going…"

The chieftess nodded. "Yes, the Pendarlon has told me. And he has said he will return to aid you."

"When?" cried Aeriel, reaching out to stay Orroto-to from going. "When will he return?"

"When you are healed," the woman answered. "Lie down now and rest. I must go work on the new walking stick I am carving, and you must not disturb the poultice on your neck." Then she turned and ducked gracefully out from under the canopy.

"How long?" insisted Aeriel. Already her head swam from sitting.

Orroto-to paused and turned, gave a slight shrug, and shook her head. "He comes when he comes," she replied. "He did not say how long. Rest now, little pale one, and patience. You must wait."

AERIEL WAITED. THE MA'A-MBAI MOVED by day with only brief stops for rest and water.

Solstar slowly reached its zenith and descended, set. The Planet waxed. As nightshade settled down, the Ma'a-mbai made camp and lived off their stores, wove, mended tools, and sang stories. They were great singers of tales beside their white fires, some reciting ancient verses while others blew on soft woodwinds or tapped their walking sticks and tambours. Aeriel heard strange tales of all the peoples of the world, and of ancient days on Oceanus as well.

But her favorite was a desert tale, the song of the Youth-Who-Tried-to-Give-Up-His-Walking-Stick. But every time he pretended to forget it and left it behind, it came skipping and jigging over the sand in pursuit. Until it had rapped him soundly on the head three times, shouting, "What are you doing? Don't you know I am yours? If I did not run after you, you'd just have to come back and find me!"—this until the youth learned that some things it is wise not to lay down. Hearing this tale by the cookfires late that first fortnight, Aeriel had laughed till her sides were sore.

At last long nightshade passed and Solstar rose. The Ma'a-mbai took up their wandering again. The wound on Aeriel's neck had healed over in a smooth, white scar and she found herself able to walk with the train the length of each march without tiring. Orroto-to gave her a carved walking stick then and taught her to stalk the cautious desert creatures: hares and deer and dusthens.

Soon Aeriel could throw deftly enough to fell quarry at ninety paces—giving her staff, when she launched it, that peculiar flick of the wrist which the chieftess had shown her, a flick which caused the arcing shaft to reverse itself with a snap in midflight, bringing its heavy, knotted crown down in a hard, swift stroke. After that Aeriel brought what game she could to the cookfires, and no longer held back when sharing in her hosts' food.

Solstar rose and set three times while Aeriel remained with the Ma'a-mbai. The days were long, the nights cool and pleasant, but at last she grew weary with the waiting. A change had overtaken her in the desert where all is patience and peace. She felt fitter, freer, stronger, surer. And her body was losing some of its youthful boniness. For the first time she felt she was beginning to resemble a maid beneath her kirtle, and not a stick-doll made of spindletwigs.

There were other changes, too. Once she had remarked to Orroto-to, "Chieftess, are you darker than when I first came?" and the woman had laughed, saying, "No, but Solstar is burning you pale." And another time Aeriel had asked her,

"Orroto-to, are you shorter than when I first met you?" but again the chieftess laughed. "No, little one. You are growing taller."

But time fast was fleeting away. Aeriel had been all of three day-months with the Ma'a-mbai, and in another two, the icarus would fly to find his final bride. Dawn was coming up for the fourth time since she had left the castle of the vampyre, when she said to the leader of the desert people, "I am going. I can wait no more on the Pendarlon. If I must find the Avarclon myself, so I must. Even now I may be too late."

Orroto-to nodded and gazed at her with her wise, dark eyes. "You are free," she said. "You must do as you must. If your walking stick has been lying too long, you should take it up again, and go where it leads. I will send the Pendarlon after you, when he comes."

Aeriel could think of no word for thanks. The chieftess nodded to her slightly, the only gesture of farewell her people had, then turned back to the Ma'a-mbai. Their procession began slowly to move on. Aeriel raised her staff to them, then turned north toward Oceanus, and began to walk. She had not been walking many hours when she heard the padding of paws in the sand behind her.

She turned as the Pendarlon bounded up beside her.

"You are an impatient one, daughter," he said. "I sought the Ma'a-mbai only to find you gone."

"Why did you wait so long to come?" Aeriel asked him as he fell into walking slowly beside her. "My wound healed all of two day-months ago."

"That is not the only wound you were healing of, daughter," the leosol replied. "But if you are fully rested now, I will take you to the Avarclon."

Aeriel nodded; the lyon bowed his head and she saw she was to mount. Putting her wrist through the braided loop at the head of her walking stick and adjusting the thong of the black velvet bag about her neck, Aeriel rested her hands on the Pendarlon's shaggy shoulders and slid onto his back.

"Hold to my mane, now," he said, and with a great bound, they were off across the dunes swifter than a greyhound. The lyon ran in bounds so long and smooth there was no jolt at all when he touched the ground and sprang again. Aeriel held to two great hanks of his fiery gold hair, which was silky and soft as satinflax.

The horizon rose and dipped at every stride.

The lyon was running straight for Oceanus, which ascended slowly but visibly. Aeriel at length grew tired of sitting and, her arms wrapped tight around his massive neck, she lay down along his back and closed her eyes. Perhaps she slept.

They ran for hours over the dunes. Rested, Aeriel pulled herself into a sitting position on the lyon's back again. Later, she ate and slept again. The leosol never slackened his pace or paused to rest. They ran past the ruins of fantastic domed cities—dark as burned-out lanterns, their domes cracked and scored with age. Once, on the far horizon she thought she saw one city that was alight, but it disappeared from view as the Pendarlon touched down, and she could not find it again when they once more rose into the air.

They ran past the bones of great animals long dead—even their skeletons were oxidizing and falling into powder. They ran past living animals, too—little lithe antelope, and great, shaggy double-humped camels. Several times she spotted kites, sailing slowly overhead, and at one point a pair of four-footed creatures watching her and the leosol intently from far away.

They looked like long-legged, huge-eared dogs with hairy tails, but when Aeriel mentioned them to the lyon, asking what they were, he merely glanced over his shoulder at them, rumbled low and darkly, once, then quickened his pace. The spotted dog-creatures loped away to the north-westward and disappeared. Aeriel forgot about them as she caught sight of a caravan to the west—a long line of riders and pack animals snaking over the dunes.

And once they passed very close to the camp of desert wanderers much like the Ma'a-mbai, save that their loose, sleeveless smocks were of pale blue instead of white. From them went up a great shout when they sighted the Pendarlon from afar. They chanted and waved their lank, knobbed walking staves, while the youths and maidens began an homage dance—bowing low to the ground and trilling a long, high song. The leosol roared mightily in answer, but never slackened his pace. Aeriel watched them recede in the distance, and their chanting and trilling hung in her ears for a long time after.

Oceanus rose higher in the heavens. The hours drifted by. Earth shrank to a fingernail crescent as the sun ascended toward its noon eclipse. Aeriel slept again, and ate from her food-sack. She lost count of the times she ate and slept. The lyon never tired.

But at last, at last when the Planet hung at

zenith in the star-crowded sky and Solstar was just
nudging at its side, then the lyon's gait began to
slacken. His breathing was as quiet and steady as
ever, but he ran more leisurely now; Aeriel knew
they were nearing the Avarclon. She looked for
him, and listened. The last of the sun slid into
eclipse.

And then she saw him across the dunes. He
was of dark silver, fiercesome and free, with a
keen horn on his forehead and two great wings
upon his shoulders; there were little wings upon
his fetlocks, and beneath his ears behind the
cheeks. He galloped toward them over sandhill
and dune, then pitched to a standstill, snorting and
stamping the ground. He let go a wild whinny
that pealed like a bugle blast. The lyon came
smoothly to a stop and roared in answer. The
sound thundered like mountains shifting, rolling
far and away, off into the distance over the dunes.

Oceanus hung huge and umbrous in the sky.
The hiding sun made a bright hallow around it.
Avarclon and Pendarlon faced each other across
the sand and cried their greetings. The darkened
sun stood so directly overhead that neither of them
cast any shade. Aeriel slid from the lyon's back
and laid her walking stick on the sand, stood be-

side the great cat beneath the eerie half-light of noon.

"How are you, my old friend?" cried the leosol.

"Well enough, considering," the starhorse replied. "And who is this you have brought with you? It has been many a day-month since last I saw any living creature but yourself."

Aeriel folded her hands and bowed, as she had been accustomed to do before the satrap whenever he had come to the syndic's house to visit his half-sister. And breathing deep, Aeriel caught a keen, clean scent like oil of silvermint. "My name is Aeriel, my lord," she said, "and I come from the castle of the vampyre...."

She got no further, for at the mention of the icarus, the starhorse shied and whinnied as if challenged. Aeriel was too startled to continue.

"Go on," the lyon told her quietly. The starhorse was, it seemed, as fierce and skittish as the leosol was strong and steady.

"Talb the duarough sent me," said Aeriel. "I do not know his real name."

"Ah, the Little Mage of the Caves of Downwending," the equustel said, tossing his head and snorting. "So he did not go with the queen to

Westernesse. Had I known I had such an ally in the plains, I might have called on him at need. Tell me, little one, why have you come?"

"He has sent me," said Aeriel, "to sing you a rime he has found in the Book of the Dead. He says you will know the meaning thereof."

The starhorse nodded, champing and sidling restlessly. "Sing me the rime," he said.

Aeriel told him:

> "On Avaric's white plain
> > where the icarus now wings
> To steeps of Terrain
> > from tour-of-the-kings,
>
> And damozels twice-seven
> > his brides have all become:
> A far cry from heaven
> > and a long road from home—
>
> Then strong-hoof of the starhorse
> > must hallow him unguessed
> If adamant's edge is to plunder
> > his breast.
>
> Then, only, may the Warhorse
> > and Warrior arise
> To rally the warhosts, and thunder
> > the skies."

The equustel nickered softly and grew suddenly gentle. Beside her, Aeriel thought she caught the faint rumbling of the lyon's purr.

"Yes, child, yes," the starhorse exclaimed. "I have heard that song before. It was one of the riddles sung over me at my making. I know its meaning well."

"Your making?" said Aeriel in wonder. "Are you not mortal? Were you not born?"

The starhorse laughed, whinnied and shook his head for sheer exuberance. "The Old Ones made *me*, child, and the lyon, and the hippogriff of the eastern steeps and the gryphon of Terrain—and the great she-wolf of forested Bern, and the lithe serpent of the Sea-of-Dust." His eyes grew bright and far; he breathed deep. "Made these and the other Wardens-of-the-World. Ravenna, Ravenna! She was a wise woman."

The Pendalon had sat down purring on the sand near Aeriel, began nibbling and licking his paw. The equustel reared and danced where he stood.

"Ravenna?" ventured Aeriel. "Who is Ravenna?"

The Avarclon whinnied fiercely and the sunlion roared.

"Ravenna, Ravenna, the Ancient who made

us," the starhorse replied. "When I was but a
fledgling foal and the Pendarlon a cub, and all
the other lons but hatchlings or whelps, then she
sang over us a song for each—a destiny to strive
after. It would come to pass, she said, if our
hearts proved true enough and fate ran fair." The
Avarclon rose and pawed the air with his hooves;
his great grey wings beat like a bird's. "Oh, she
was learnèd, and steadfast, and kind. She foresaw
the great changes that were to pass—even the
coming of the icari, and how they might be
undone."

"Tell me of the Old Ones," Aeriel begged him.
Curiosity burned in her to know.

Then the Avarclon nodded and Aeriel sat down
on the sand near the leosol to listen, while the
starhorse spoke to her of ancient days, of the coming of the Ancients into the world, plunging across
the heavens from Oceanus in chariots of fire, how
they brought air and water and life to the land,
bred plants and made creatures to populate it, then
fashioned all the peoples of the world. Aeriel was
stolen away with wonder at his tale, and the starhorse seemed to grow more beautiful and spirited
as the eclipse reached its fullest.

But then he spoke of great wars and plagues on

Oceanus, of the departure for their homeland of all but a few of the Heaven-born. Then the chariots ceased coming, and gradually the land began to change; most of the water ran off into the ground and the atmosphere began to thin. Species of plants and animals died out. One by one, the Ancients sealed themselves off in their domed cities and refused to have more to do with the slowly dying planet. Left to themselves, the people fell into tribalism.

Ravenna had been the last to go, to disappear into her domed city, sealed away from further commerce with the world. But before she had gone—and she would not say why she was going—she had fashioned the wardens, more than a dozen of them, to watch over the various quarters, protecting the people and keeping the peace until such time, lost far into the indefinite future, that she had promised to return.

And the wardens had kept their ranges well for almost a thousand years—until the coming of the icari. No creature seemed able to stand against them. Six lons already had fallen to the six that had come so far, and now this last, the seventh, was in Avaric. And when he joined their ranks as a true vampyre and made their number complete, it was said, then they meant to fly in force against the other kingdoms, and take all the world in their teeth.

And to Aeriel, swept away by the starhorse's words, it seemed for a moment that her heart was no longer her own. She sensed the equustel's cold hatred for the vampyre and his brethren, the sunlion's more heated ire. She felt the same outrage well up in her own breast against the icari—be they ever so fair—as at last she comprehended the full malevolence of their intent. She stared at the starhorse in dismay. "But why have you abandoned Avaric to the darkangel?" she cried.

The Avarclon gave a low horse-laugh that sounded bitterly amused. "Daughter, you speak as though you believe I gladly left. Child, I am exiled unwilling. Do you not think I would return to vanquish the vampyre if I could?" The greathorse shook his head. "He has proven too strong for me, and my fate is left unfulfilled." He gazed off across the rolling dunes toward Avaric. "Though neither could he destroy me, nor would I let him catch me to enslave me—so he has driven me out with his terrible might."

The words had greatly saddened him. He paused for breath. Above them, the eclipse was nearing its close. In a moment, Solstar would peer from behind the Planet.

"But now," said Aeriel, "the time is ripe. Soon he will take his fourteenth bride and be master absolute of the plain. You must come back with me. Is it not written that by the hoof of the starhorse the vampyre shall fall? Come back with me."

The Avarclon shook his head slowly. He looked visibly weaker than he had only a few minutes before. His head drooped. His coat no longer shone. He seemed to grow gaunt before her eyes.

"If only I could, child," he whispered, his voice growing thin and hoarse. "If only..."

The rim of the sun slid from behind Oceanus. Light spilled over the dunes. The Avarclon gave a low moan of despair. His eyes were dull and glazed. His flesh shrank and melted away beneath the skin. Aeriel saw his bones.

"What is it?" she cried softly. "What is happening?"

"Hush, child," said the lyon. "He cannot hear you now."

The starhorse moaned again and shuddered. "Avaric!" he cried. "Avaric, Avaric!"

His legs grew stick-thin and buckled. He pitched forward onto the sand. Aeriel gasped and pressed closer to the lyon.

"Tell me what is happening," she begged him. "I'm afraid."

The grey horse struggled to rise. His wings thrashed desperately. His legs folded under him like a newborn colt's. His second attempt was weaker. His third weaker still. His wings ceased beating. He gave a deep sigh; his head bowed slowly, slowly till his nose just touched the ground. His rib cage heaved and his breath stirred the sand.

"Each of us," the lyon said, "each of the wardens is bound to the lands we ward. None of us can spend many day-months from our domains without..."

Aeriel hardly heard the rest. Solstar was halfway out from behind the Planet. The starhorse aged before her eyes. He no longer struggled to rise, or even to keep his head up, but just to keep himself upright. He swayed, righted himself, swayed again. At last he lost the battle and rolled slowly over on his side. His long, graceless legs kicked, writhed; his head moved feebly in the sand. His jet eye stared at the sky above. Aeriel could see white Solstar reflected in it.

Then his eye darkened, and even the reflected light in it went out. He lay still. His flesh moldered and crumbled. His moth-eaten skin hung in rags from the bone. The tatters sagged in the slight wind, tiny pennants. Then they, too, were gone and only the hard things were left—teeth, bones, hooves, and horn, and a few strands of his mane and tail, and the feathers of his wings. The desert wind sighed softly; some of the feathers drifted away across the dunes.

"He is dead!" cried Aeriel, unable even now quite to believe it. "Why did you do nothing? What killed him?"

"Exile killed him. He tried many times to return to the plains. Each time the vampyre drove him back at the border. He has not set hoof in Avaric for twelve years."

"He has been here twelve years?" said Aeriel. "But I thought..."

The lyon nodded. "It is just as I said. He has been dead twelve years."

"But," Aeriel began, "I saw him living...."

The Pendarlon shook his head. "Daughter, have you never heard that phantoms walk at noon?"

Aeriel looked at the heap of bleached bone on the dune before her. The slight desert wind breathed soft against her skin, lifted her hair. She gazed at her feet. She felt empty of a sudden, and utterly alone. Her quest had failed; the starhorse was dead. She heaved a little sigh, felt starved for air. Her heart hurt; her throat hurt.

"Then it is hopeless," she whispered, "and it was hopeless from the first. Why did you not tell me at once that he was dead?"

"Because it makes no matter," said the Pendarlon.

"No matter?" cried Aeriel. "The starhorse is fallen. He cannot come back with me. Now the darkangel can never be vanquished, and I cannot save his wives. All is lost, and I have failed."

"Nothing is lost," the lyon said, "nor have you failed. Sing me the rime again."

Aeriel did so, repeating it dully:

"On Avaric's white plain
　　　　　where the icarus now wings
To steeps of Terrain
　　　　　from tour-of-the-kings,

And damozels twice-seven
　　　　　his brides have all become;
A far cry from heaven
　　　　　and a long road from home—

Then strong-hoof of the starhorse
must hallow him..."

She was midway through the third coupling
when the Pendarlon stopped her. "There. That
line. Say it over."

Aeriel drew breath and started to repeat it.
" 'Then strong-hoof of the starhorse must...' "

"Ah, child," the lyon cried, "do you not see?
The hoof, the hoof is your prize—not the equustel
himself."

Aeriel stared at the warden before her and wondered if of a sudden he could have gone mad. She
shook her head to clear it, tried to find her tongue
again. "Pendarlon, what do you mean?"

A laugh purred deep in the lyon's throat. "You
have but to take his hoof, daughter, and your
quest is done."

Surely his manner was not mad, she reflected,
uncertainly, though his words made no sense to
her. She glanced at the skeleton of the Avarclon.
Abruptly, she remembered the duarough's words:
"Seek after the starhorse—he of the strong hoof,
undying. Bring back what you may of him, for it
is by the hoof of the starhorse that the icarus will
fall." *Bring back what you may of him.* At the time
she had thought he must mean news.

She stood a moment, indecisive. Could the little mage have meant the horse's hoof? Aeriel snorted; and yet she had already seen and heard of stranger things. If only he had had time to explain! The Pendarlon sat watching her as she eyed the hooves of the skeleton. Well, there could be no harm, at least, in taking one. Still she felt uneasy.

"I cannot rob the dead," she told him.

"The dead are dead," the leosol replied. "They have given up their bodies. He will not mind that you borrow his hoof for a little. Truly, you may do more good than you know by it."

He started across the dune toward the starhorse. Aeriel hesitated.

"Come, daughter," he said, glancing to northwestward. "We must away before much longer, or I shall not get you back to the border by nightfall."

Aeriel stood a moment, wondered on the direction of his glance. Their way home lay south. She followed him to the scattered bones. Kneeling in the sand, she murmured, "Which hoof?"

"The forehoof on the near side," said the leosol.

Aeriel grasped it gently and it came off in her hand. The other hooves were dull grey, almost leaden in hue. The one in her hand, however, was bright and gleamed like some precious metal. Aeriel held it cupped in her hand a long moment, gazing at it. "But how?" she wondered aloud. "What virtue is there in this hoof now?"

"Come, child," said the Pendarlon, with another glance to the western north. "The duarough will know."

Aeriel opened the mouth of her black velvet bag and slid the hoof inside. She drew the mouth closed and let the pouch drop limp and empty-seeming against her breast beneath her smock. Solstar blazed down. Taking her walking stick in hand once more, she turned to the lyon and mounted his back. He wheeled swift as lightning and sprang away in a lithe leap over the dunes. They rose into the air and touched down, rose and touched down. The lyon ran in long, tireless strides, and soon they had left the equustel far behind.

TEN

The Witch's Dogs

AERIEL AND THE LYON SET OFF ACROSS
the sand, traveling southward, away from the center of the world and toward the border of the
plain. But it seemed to Aeriel, as she sat or lay
along the leosol's back, ate or slept or gazed at
the endless dunes beneath the stars, that a subtle
difference was present now. Some aspect of the
lyon's stride, or breath, or the flexing of muscles
along his back betrayed tension. Though the
Pendarlon said never a word, Aeriel found herself
now and again glancing back to scan the dunes
behind, marked by the lyon's trail of pawprints
over the sand.

They were little more than halfway to the borderland when Aeriel spotted their pursuers. Solstar
had declined midway toward the east horizon.
What she saw were then no more than white

specks far, a very long way behind them and loping eastward out of the western north. At first Aeriel thought nothing of them, guessing whatever they were—be it loping dogs or deer or long-legged running birds—would cross her and the lyon's trail far back, at a slant, and continue on to the east. Then she saw one of the creatures—still no more than a pale dot—stop dead behind them over the lyon's tracks and heard it sing out a strange, savage-sweet cry, as if calling its fellows to trail.

Even from afar, the cry reached faintly, clearly to Aeriel's ears. She felt the lyon suddenly tense; he jerked his head around. "Odds," she heard him rumble, "I was afraid of that—that those two might be to their mistress and back before I could get you safely to the plain."

"Back?" said Aeriel. She could not remember having seen such a pack of creatures before. And there were more than two, at least a dozen of them fallen in behind the leading pair and coursing down the trail. They were still too far for her to make out clearly what they were. "Pendarlon, what are they?"

But the lyon only said, "Hold tight, daughter, and let me save my breath for running. Happily, if we can lose them, you will not need to know."

His answer puzzled her, frightened her. Aeriel buried her forearms in the leosol's fiery mane, tightened her knees as the sunlion launched into a faster pace. The wind whipped at her. Aeriel pressed herself against the Pendarlon, glanced back. Their pursuers had gained a little, were near enough now for Aeriel to see they were four-footed and smaller than the great cat by several times. She turned back to the lyon.

"But why do we flee, then?" she cried in his ear. "Are you not Pendarlon, and every natural denizen of this region your ally?"

She heard the leosol laugh, a hard-edged laugh with no humor in it. "Ah, these are no natural creatures, daughter. They belong to the white witch of the lake."

"The lake?" said Aeriel slowly, more to herself than to him. Memory stirred. "A still, dead lake in the middle of a canyon—at desert's western edge?" She remembered the story Dirna had told her, the last tale she had told the darkangel. "But what business has this witch with you?"

"She seeks to rule my ward," replied the lyon, panting, "as the icarus now rules Avaric." Despite his shortness of breath, his tone was low and measured. "She has dwelt in that lake since before my making and cannot be driven out, but though she herself is confined to its waters, she sends her spials and catspaws out over my desert, working her mischief—I kill them when I can."

Aeriel let out her own breath then, realized she had been holding it. She felt cold, leaned closer to the sunlion's warmth.

"But now," the Pendarlon was saying, "I think I would rather outrun these than fight. I have you to look after—and your prize."

Aeriel eased her grip on the lyon just long enough to touch the little black velvet bag that hung, still empty-seeming, from the thong about her neck. Her heavy-knobbed walking stick lay slung from her wrist, tapping against her leg and side as the leosol sped. Aeriel turned again to look behind her, and her heart recoiled. Gradually, steadily, the witch's creatures were lessening the space between themselves and their quarry. Solstar had traveled three times its own diameter farther toward horizon's edge when they drew close enough for Aeriel to make out clearly what they were.

They looked to her like long-legged dogs, with great upright ears, massy, humping shoulders, and whisk-hair tails. They were pale, very pale in color, a ghostly hue that shone like dim earth-shine. And they were spotted, their backs and sides covered with broken rosettes like those of pards—blots the blackness of an ermine's eye, or a starless night, or a darkangel's wings. Aeriel shivered suddenly, realizing she had seen two such creatures before, from a distance, as the lyon had borne her to the equustel.

They ran in two long lines of a half-dozen each, these dogs, flanking the leosol's trail. The lines alternately lengthened and bunched—never stable, never steady. Their members constantly sprang sideways, over each other's backs as they ran, changing places, like gazelles. The luminous pallor of their coats hung like haze before Aeriel's vision; the darkness of their spots seemed to shimmer and shift. She found she could watch them only in glances, or her head began to ache and her stomach stir uneasily.

They were singing a song as they came, a crooning that soared and dropped suddenly down scales with never a pause for breath. It made Aeriel's ears ring. But it was only when they had drawn even closer that Aeriel noticed their eyes. Intense and angry red as carbuncles they glowed —eyes with neither iris, nor pupil, nor lid.

Aeriel shrank away from them against the lyon. Seeing her, their pursuers yipped and yapped with laughter, slavering and snapping their jaws. "Jackals," Aeriel whispered. "Jackals, jackals."

"Aye, daughter," the lyon nodded. His breath was coming shorter now. "The witch's dogs."

"Can we go no faster?" Aeriel cried, clutching him. "They are fairly nipping at your heels."

The pale, bounding jackals gave another bark of glee, and Aeriel realized their great, pricked ears must be able to hear even her tight-throated whisper.

The leosol turned his head. "Not, I fear, and keep you aboard," he told her quietly. Aeriel felt her desperation rising. Her limbs already ached with the strain of resisting the wind. The Pendarlon eyed the gaining dogs, then Solstar, then the stars. "Daughter, I had hoped to get you safe across the border," he rumbled at last. "These creatures take great mastery to wield at any distance from the witch's mere, and her might is much weakened by desert's edge.... But pah," he snorted angrily, "I think we shall have to face them now."

Aeriel felt herself pale. The jackals hooted and snatched at the air with their teeth. The leosol growled.

"But hold fast to me first," he bade her. "If

face them we must, let us at least choose our own ground."

With that, he sprang away suddenly in such an unaccustomed burst of speed that Aeriel was dizzied. She locked her arms, her legs about him. Behind them the jackals sent up a wild yell—not of dismay but as of triumph. Their hunting song grew suddenly bolder, fiercer. Turning, Aeriel saw the double line of red-eyed dogs dashing in pursuit.

The wind buffeting her was so intense Aeriel could scarcely breathe. She felt her hands slipping on the lyon's hot, silk mane, her knees dragging along his side as the rush of air shoved her back from his shoulders. Gritting her teeth and clenching her eyes, she clasped him as hard as she could. Even that was not enough. She felt herself beginning to slip....

The lyon stopped—smoothly, without jolt, but instantly. Aeriel clung to him, dazed. Her body felt numb in the sudden cessation of wind. She gasped for breath. "Quick, daughter," the great cat was crying, shrugging his shoulders to help her off, "to the ground. We must stand ready."

Aeriel tumbled to the sand, knelt a moment on hands and knees, winded. The leosol had brought them partway up the steep lee side of a dune. The lee slope slanted sharply away in front of them, toward the oncoming jackals. Behind her Aeriel saw the top of the same slope recurving to hang above her and the Pendarlon like the crest of a frozen wave—preventing attack from the rear. Aeriel scrambled to her feet and pulled her walking stick from her wrist. The lyon had already faced about toward the double line of jackals coursing up the slope.

"Remember, daughter," the lyon said as she took her place beside him. "Stand flank to flank with me and do not let them part us. Odds," he growled in undertone, seemingly more to himself than to her, "a pair or even four of them would be no hard task to dispatch—but so many! I have never seen the like." Aeriel stood breathing fast and deeply, to steady herself. Gripping her staff, she gazed at the swiftly approaching pack. Beside her the Pendarlon snorted, shook his head. "Faith," he murmured, "their mistress's might must be growing vast."

The witch's dogs loped to within ten paces of the leosol and halted. The two leaders came a few paces farther, then sat, regarding their quarry with hot, deep red eyes while the rest of the pack milled and trotted behind them, leaping over one another in a disturbing confusion of light and dark. Aeriel turned her eyes from them, studied the leaders instead. The one on the left, nearest the leosol, was slimmer, a female; her brawnier companion across from Aeriel, a male.

They licked their lips and panted, waiting. Aeriel fingered her walking stick nervously, wondered which end might make the better weapon: the knotted head or the pointed heel. All the while, the weaving pack never gave up their high, humming song. Then the shaggy jackal spoke to the Pendarlon, ignoring Aeriel.

"So, lyon," he said, grinning. "So." Gloating made his voice thick. His white-dark coat shimmered eerily. Behind him, the witch's pack-dogs prowled; half were heavy-shouldered like himself, the others slighter, like the brach beside him. "Give up your rider to us, lyon," the jackal said. "Our mistress wants her."

Aeriel's eyes widened. They wanted *her*? She had thought they pursued the Pendarlon. She heard the leosol rumbling deep in his throat. "By our lady Ravenna," he answered, low and dangerous, "I am unaccustomed to obeying *your* commands." Aeriel racked her wits. What could the water witch of that desert lake want with her? The Pendarlon growled at the dogs, "I kill your kind."

The jackal cut him off. "Ah, but that is all in

the past, now, lyonling, when you came upon us singly, or in pairs. Now we in a pack have run you down, and you know very well you cannot stand against us." He rose and arched his back lazily, stretching. "Still, it is not you we want today. Only your passenger. Give her up to us, or we'll take her."

The rumble in the Pendarlon's throat grew darker, halfway between a purr and a growl, sounded to Aeriel like the dull thunder of approaching hooves. An answering growl arose from the jackal's throat. He lowered his head. Aeriel tensed. But then the other jackal, the brach, slunk forward a pace or two.

"But softly now," she mused. Behind her the others wove and leapfrogged. Above their hunting song, they whined impatiently, licked their teeth. "Why always conflict," said the brach, "when simple persuasion may suffice?" Her round, lidless eyes gleamed red and cunning. "Come, cat," she murmured to the Pendarlon, "why resist? Hand over your prize willingly and you will earn our lady's gratitude. Join us!" Her voice grew softer still, even more winning. "Our mistress can grant you whatever you desire...."

"The one thing I desire, jackal-brach," the lyon roared, "is to see your mistress overthrown!"

All the jackals fell back snarling. Aeriel herself flinched at the force of the Pendarlon's words. "Fool," hissed the witch's dog; her companions gathered themselves. "Cat. Fool."

Then, of a sudden, the jackals sprang. Half lunged for the leosol, half for Aeriel. Catching up her walking stick near the pointed base, Aeriel swung its heavy knobbed crown in a wide arc almost before she had time to think. The witch's dogs ducked, fell back, and sprang again. Again Aeriel swung and once more the jackals shied just out of reach.

To the side of her Aeriel heard the lyon fending off his own attackers with savage growls and swipes of his paw. Aeriel kept her eyes on the pack before her. As they regrouped, still humming above the snarls, still bounding, weaving, and staring at her with their carbuncle eyes, she realized how they had bunched themselves.

The quick, slender braches all dodged and darted about the lyon, ducking under his guard one at a time to worry him with their teeth. Casting a brief glance in his direction, Aeriel saw golden blood streaking the whiteness of his coat. The slower, more powerful dog-jackals faced Aeriel.

She gripped her walking staff, watching them

intently, trying to follow their movements despite the confusing shimmer of light and dark. Her clenched fingers hurt. Then suddenly, almost before she could react, one of the jackals lunged at her. Aeriel cried out, stumbled back, jabbed with her walking stick—too slowly. A scream escaped her throat as the jackal's jaws closed over her wrist.

She felt no pain, no crunch of bone, nothing. Aeriel stared. The jackal's teeth met, passed through her like vapor. Her staff, as she thrust it, met no resistance, glided through her attacker's chest and shoulders as through empty air. She heard the dog-jackals' yipping, snarling laughter. The one before her fell back grinning, growling. Aeriel stood as if knocked breathless, staring at her whole, unwounded wrist.

"Lyon," she stammered. "Pendarlon, what is it?" Her jackals crouched back from her in a semicircle, barking in gleeful, red-eyed malice. "It passed through my hand. My stick went right through—what manner of beast are they?"

The leosol glanced over one shoulder and stared at her, startled—but only for a moment. His pack of jackals had not paused, even to taunt him with laughter. Aeriel saw more blood on the lyon's coat, though for the most part he seemed to be keeping the braches at bay with furious snaps of his jaw and powerful sweeps of his paw.

"Specters!" he cried suddenly. "Daughter, I should have seen it...."

Now it was Aeriel's turn to stare. "Specters," she murmured. Her mind seemed too dulled to take it in. It came to her slowly then, memory of Bomba's cradle tales with their specters: images without substance, able to be seen and heard, but neither touched nor felt.... Aeriel shook her head, catching sight once more of the sunlion's golden blood. "But you are wounded," she exclaimed. "How could they have harmed you?"

Her jackals had begun to mill and circle again, heads lowered, grinning. Aeriel brandished her stick, wondered what good that would do. The witch-dogs redoubled their mocking laughter.

"Desert jackals only run in pairs, daughter," panted the Pendarlon, keeping his own attackers back. "I grasp it now. The witch could not have had time to assemble all her jackals, nor has she power to control them all so far from her." One of the braches came too close. Aeriel caught a glimpse of the lyon's paw passing through her solid-seeming body. "Only two of this pack can be real," the lyon muttered, "the rest created in their images to confound us."

He cuffed at another brach-jackal and his paw met only empty air. Only two of the pack were real, had he said? thought Aeriel. His bright blood gleamed from the flesh wounds on his shoulders and forelegs. But those two real dogs were obviously dangerous, and lost in this shifting crowd— "How may we find them?" she cried. All the dog-jackals prowling before her looked exactly alike, as did the braches.

"We cannot," gasped the lyon, lunging and feinting. "She has made perfect likenesses. We dare not disregard any one of them lest..." His last words ended in a snarl. Aeriel turned in time to see one of the brach-jackals—the real one, clearly—sink her teeth into the great cat's pad, draw blood, then dodge out of reach before he could knock her away.

They're just toying with us, thought Aeriel, for sport. They could have finished up long since, did they not so joy in baiting us.

Aeriel felt a sudden rush of motion along her side and realized she had dropped her guard. Something hot and sharp grazed her forearm. She whirled away with a cry, bringing her knotted stick down on solid, shaggy bulk. She heard a yip of pain, surprise, and the dog-jackal fell quickly back, head low, blank lidless eyes glowering at her.

He is the one, thought Aeriel. Her heart lifted; she ignored the pain of the gash along her arm. If I can but keep my eye on him...

She aimed another blow of her staff at the witch's dog. But he fell back from her, deliberately, lost himself in the shifting shimmer of his fellows. Aeriel could not keep her eyes on him in the dance of spots. The jackals sang their hunting song and laughed. Aeriel halted, afraid to advance more than a pace from the lyon's side lest one slip behind her.

Aeriel heard a sharp yelp from one of the Pendarlon's jackals, glanced to see a brach tumbling away from the leosol's mighty paw. For an instant all the other braches vanished. Downslope, the brach he had struck—the real one—staggered to her feet, one forepaw crumpled to her chest, and shook her head.

Her fellows suddenly reappeared, barking and lunging about the lyon's ears, to no effect. He had the real one in his sight and she was injured, could not leap and lose herself among the others. Aeriel saw the great cat belly down to the sand and move fluidly forward. His golden blood gleamed in the light of Solstar.

Blood on the teeth, thought Aeriel suddenly, returning her mind to her own fight now. Only a real jackal can harm me; only the real one has wounded me. Her slashed arm ached. The real witch-dog, Aeriel realized, must have my blood on his teeth. She searched the miasma of roving red eyes and broken black spots before her, tried to find fangs, stared at them—yes. One of the jackals did have a smear of rose on his white curled lip.

He stood out from the others now as she recognized how to spot him. And she realized, too, as she studied him, that only he cast a shadow across the orange sand. Gripping her walking stick, she darted toward him, landed three quick blows to his head and shoulders. He barked, snarled, backed away from her. She followed, ignoring the howling pack of specters that sprang at her. She waded through their nothingness and aimed again at the one witch-dog she knew was real.

"Stop," the jackal growled at her. He crouched, shoulders hunched; no laughter thickened his voice now. Abruptly the noise of the others ceased. Their images vanished. Aeriel was dimly aware in the sudden stillness that the false braches about the Pendarlon had also vanished. "Enough," the jackal crouching before her snarled. "You recognize I am the one. Very well. I shall stop toying with you. Even without my specters, I can kill you. Do you really think that stick would stop me?"

"The Pendarlon will soon finish with your mate," panted Aeriel. Despite the other's surly confidence, she felt flushed and dangerous. "Do you think you could stand against him?"

"I said, enough!" the jackal snarled. "I do not intend to stand against him. I intend to kill you and run. Have done with this game and save yourself death. Hand over to me the starhorse's hoof."

Aeriel stared at him, startled. Was it the star-hoof they truly sought, not her? She felt a brief rush of gratification flit through her to realize perhaps she had done right in taking the hoof, interpreted the rime and the little mage's hurried instructions correctly after all. She blinked once to clear her thoughts, and searched her mind for cunning. "And...and what if I had this thing you ask for," she started, trying for a tone of confidence, even scorn; she was winded. She needed rest. "What would you do with it?"

"There is no 'if,'" the jackal barked. "The lyon took you to the horse: so much we can guess. What other reason than to have its hoof? I and my fellow servants have been scouring these dunes a dozen years to find it. . . ."

"But why?" demanded Aeriel, stalling, stalling—would the lyon never come? From one corner of her eye she caught sight of him, now halfway down the slope, almost caught up to the limping, fleeing brach.

"Our mistress requires it," the dog-jackal snapped, baring fang. "Ask no more. Hand it to me."

Aeriel shook her head, slowly, held tight her walking stick, her muscles tensed, eyes on the jackal—but she made her face and voice all ignorance. "I do not have it," she replied. "This robe has no pockets." She raised her arms slightly to show him. "Did you think I might secrete anything upon my person?" The jackal cocked his head, eyed her with red suspicion. Aeriel dropped her arms. "I brought back nothing of the starhorse. He was dead."

"Liar," spat the jackal. "You have it—you must—somewhere upon you. That pouch . . ."

Aeriel lifted the black velvet bag, still slung from a thong about her neck, prayed for the lyon to come. She wrung the limp bag in one hand. "It holds nothing." In the background she heard the death cry of the brach in the lyon's jaws.

"Liar," the witch-dog growled again, his muscles bunching, his eyes upon the pouch. "More likely charmed and only empty-seeming—"

He sprang—so suddenly Aeriel was taken by surprise. Snatching the bag in his teeth from her hand, he knocked her back. She cried out, used her staff to ward him off. Falling, she felt the thong break from about her neck. The hard sand knocked the breath from her. The jackal came down upon her. For one instant his red, carbuncle eyes glared at her; his hot, foul breath scathed her cheek. Then she heard the lyon's roar and the jackal sprang away.

She scrambled to her knees, saw all in an instant: the witch-dog already two bounds downslope, the Pendarlon crouching over the fallen brach. A long wound was torn along his left leg and shoulder—she had not seen that slash before; his stance during the fight had hidden it. The jackal fled.

"Pendarlon, stop him!" Aeriel cried. "He has the pouch. . . ." But she realized even as she heard herself speaking that with such a wound, even the leosol could never have caught him.

The great cat staggered to his feet, lurched half a pace toward her. "Aeriel," he called—but his voice seemed oddly weakened, strained. "Aeriel, your staff!"

But Aeriel's thoughts were already ahead of his words. Scrambling up from her knees, she snatched at her staff, lying where she had dropped it when she fell. Just out of reach, it slipped beneath her fingertips, sifted further into the coarse, slippery sand. Aeriel lunged for the stick, caught it up, whirled. She saw the pale, dark-spotted jackal, pouch in teeth, now halfway to the foot of the slope. Gauging the distance in that instant, she knew were she to wait even a half second more, he would be beyond her range and away.

Aeriel gathered herself. Without a pause, striving to recall everything Orroto-to had taught her, she flexed her arm and cocked her wrist, took two half-running strides, and threw. The knotted staff arched up, sailed high like a javelin, point first. Reaching its zenith, it hung a moment against the black, starlit sky. Then it plunged, dropped. Aeriel, standing halted, panting on the hillcrest, saw the jackal, unaware of the danger overhead, sprinting down the pale orange duneside straight for the point where the shaft would come to earth.

The thrown stick fell, fell, and just before it hit home, Aeriel's wrist-flick as she had launched it caught up with the shaft, snapped it around so the great knob of its head struck the dog's skull like a stone. Aeriel saw the jackal somersault, the black pouch fly from his teeth, and heard no cry. A great splash of sand flew up as the jackal landed, rolled limply a few paces to the slope's foot, and lay still.

"Well done, daughter." She heard the lyon's cry dimly above the harshness of her own breathing and the pounding of her heart. "Well done."

Aeriel half-ran, half-waded down the brittle-crusted, sliding slope then to retrieve the duarough's velvet bag and her walking stick. The jackal was dead. As Aeriel knelt in the sand beside him, she saw his eyes were clear now, colorless as glass and no longer red. The whiteness of his pelt, too, was losing its lambence; the once depthless black of its rosette spots had dulled, looked flat and dusty now. Her pulse and breathing quieted.

Aeriel lifted the velvet pouch and brushed the sand grains from it, reached her hand inside to be sure that the equustel's hoof was still within, and unharmed. It was; Aeriel felt its cool, smooth, uneven solidity against her fingertips. She reknotted the broken thong and slipped it once more about her neck. Retrieving her walking stick, she rose, turned away from the dead jackal, and started back up the slope.

The Pendarlon reclined upon the sand, facing away from Aeriel. The dead brach lay nearby him, her eyes, like her mate's, also gone colorless, her spotted coat likewise lost the gleam of its whiteness and the depth of its shadows. But as Aeriel drew near the reclining sunlion, she noticed another thing. His coat, too, had faded; its fiery radiance was weaker. His fallow mane no longer fiercely glowed. His own pelt, the brach beside him, and the sand all were spattered with bright golden blood.

Aeriel stared a moment in utter astonishment, then ran to him. Falling to her knees beside him, she found him barely able to raise his cheek from the sand. "Pendarlon," she cried, taking his great, shaggy head onto her lap. "Pendarlon, you're sorely hurt."

"No, daughter," he scoffed, faintly. "A little. Only a little."

"What may I do for you?" she exclaimed, reaching to press his wounded shoulder in effort to stanch the blood that oozed there. But in the next instant she had caught her hand back with a cry. The long, golden slash was hot as burning butter.

"No, do not touch my shoulder, child," the leosol told her. "Our bodies—the bodies of the lons—are not like yours. We are made of a fiercer, more volatile stuff...." His voice faded to a whisper. He drew breath. "But do not fear."

"I do, though," Aeriel told him, stroking his paled, silk mane with her free hand. Her chest was tight. Her voice trembled. "Lyon, I do fear."

He smiled, faintly, seemed to gather himself. From deep in his throat, she almost thought she heard a purr. "Do not. I will be well enough again before sun reaches noon next day-month. Ravenna gave her wardens power to heal themselves at need."

"But how may I aid you?" she whispered, already reaching to the pouch at her throat. "Do you require food?"

He shook his head. "No, but I require rest." He closed his eyes a moment, as though too weary to continue.

Aeriel felt her own helplessness knotting like a fist about her throat. "But what may *I* do?" she cried softly. "Tell."

He opened his eyes then, and she saw that their golden fire, at least, remained undimmed. It gave her courage. "Look to yourself," he told her, "first. Your arm is wounded. Salve a little of my blood upon it. It will help it heal."

Aeriel shook her head, made to protest. How could she tend her own scratches when he lay so hurt? But the lyon's eyes compelled her. Slowly, reluctantly, she spread a little of the hot substance from her hand along the long, shallow slash on her forearm. The golden stuff first burned, then tingled with a soothing warmth. "Lyon...," Aeriel started.

But again the great cat shook his head. "Daughter," he interrupted, "surely you can see I cannot bear you any farther toward the desert's edge. This wound of mine will mend in time, but I must lie here long hours in the light of Solstar, drawing strength from it, before I am sound again. You must go on alone."

"I won't leave you," Aeriel cried, almost before she herself was aware she had spoken. "Pendarlon..."

"You must," the leosol replied, and here, despite its weakness, his tone grew stern. "But a single day-month remains until the vampyre flies. In that time you must return to his keep and give the Avarclon's immortal hoof into the hands of the duarough." Aeriel felt her heart grow cold at mention of the icarus. She had hardly thought of him in many day-months. "Otherwise the dark-angel will have his final bride," the lyon said, "and all our efforts—yours, mine, the little mage's—will be undone. Is that what you would have?"

Aeriel shook her head. Her heart felt now bitten in two. She grieved to leave the lyon so, alone upon the dunes, and she feared also returning to the vampyre's keep. She bent her head over the Pendarlon. "No," she whispered. "No."

She did not realize she was weeping till she saw the tears falling upon his mane. "Peace, child," the lyon told her. "Courage."

"I have no courage," she replied. "I am not brave."

"So you continue to claim." She was not sure whether she heard a trace of amusement in his voice or not.

The leosol let her alone then, closed his eyes to rest. Aeriel let the tears fall until no more would come. Then she scrubbed the burning gold from her one hand with dry sand and found her walking stick. The Pendarlon opened his eyes. She put her arms about his shaggy neck, rested her head against his tawny mane.

"Since I must go, I shall," she whispered. "I am no help to you here." Trying to breathe smoothly now, she had not tears or strength left to weep. "Good-bye. You have helped me much."

"Farewell, daughter," the lyon said. "Do you know the way?"

"South," she answered. "Due south to desert's edge and across the plain. Pendarlon, shall ever I see you again?"

"Perhaps," the great cat said, "though much rides on chance, and the gods, and your own skill. Be off now, child, and the luck of the stars run with you."

Aeriel held to him hard for a moment, then rose and turned away. She started upslope toward the dune crest. The sand slid under her feet. The sun on her left was already two-thirds of the distance toward horizon's edge. With luck, she might reach the plains by dusk. Her shadow streamed out long and black across the dune face to her right.

She reached the crest and looked behind her. The Pendarlon lay by the fallen brach, his eyes now closed again, his breathing shallow but regular. The light of Solstar bathed him and his wounds. Aeriel would have paused to watch him if she had let herself. She wanted to. She made herself turn away and face the south, then started down the windward side of the dune.

ELEVEN

Return

AERIEL WALKED. SWIFTLY, DETERMINEDLY, she padded over the coarse, crusted sand. Her desert staff made a soft, scrunching sound as its tapered heel bit into the sand. She walked until the sun had fallen four degrees in the heavens, and when she could step no farther, let her knees buckle and lay face down in the trough between two dunes.

Sleep enveloped her at once and she dreamed of the darkangel, saw him snapping the bone of a bat's wing between his teeth while telling her, "You are even more sport to bait than these." Aeriel felt a sharp pang from the scar on her neck and stirred in her sleep. In dreams she heard the duarough's voice crying, "Haste, daughter, and find the Avarclon," though she herself protested, "I have not yet said that I shall help you."

Hollow-eyed, the wraiths drifted before her, moaning, "Aeriel, Aeriel will not help us!" She heard her own voice cry out, "Eoduin! Which one of you is Eoduin?" Then she heard the gargoyles howling and rattling their chains as Orroto-to assured her, "Peace, little pale one. Everyone is free," and the Pendarlon whispered, "I cannot bear you any farther. You must go on alone."

Aeriel awoke with a start to find herself lying alone in the empty desert. Solstar hung barely five degrees from setting. The forward edge of one drifting dune had eased gently over her feet and legs. She shoved herself to her knees and hastily batted away the soft weight of sand. Only then did she realize she was shivering. Her bones felt cold; her muscles ached. She chafed her chill limbs stiffly a moment and wondered if the vampyre would strangle her the moment she returned. Then she chewed a little of the food from her pouch, though she had no stomach for it, struggled to her feet, and started off again. It was not until many hours later—too late to retrace her steps—that she realized she had left her walking stick behind.

She reached the borderland just as Solstar touched the east horizon. She halted on the last sandy downslope, leaned back against the crusted duneside a few moments to rest. Beyond lay the loose, grey soil and scrub of the wasteland bordering the plains. The sun on her left was already half-hidden behind the eastern steeps by the time she roused herself. Solstar gradually slipped behind the mountains and the grey scrubland turned black. Aeriel walked on through the pale earthshine; the great star had been a long time set before she allowed herself again to rest.

The stars wheeled, slowly, halfway round the sky. The Planet waxed, earthblue, toward midnight, gradually waned, and the wound on her forearm mended in a long, pale scar. The fortnight passed. Aeriel trudged and rested, ate, slept, then arose again and continued on—always south. Visions of the darkangel invaded her dreams.

It was in the grey dark before dawn that Aeriel first made out the icarus' castle, mounted on its mountain jutting up from the plain. She made for it steadily, more numb than afraid, and by the time Solstar had risen, she had reached the cliff's foot. The gargoyles spotted her as the light grew bright enough. They began wailing horribly, as they had wailed when the darkangel had first brought her to keep. They sounded starved and desperate. She knew no one had fed them while she was gone.

She found the stairs cut into the cliff face, the uneven narrow stone steps leading down from the garden. Aeriel tucked the velvet pouch beneath the neck of her robe and began to ascend. The gargoyles continued their screaming. She knew the vampyre must have heard them by now.

Suddenly, she saw him. He stood at garden's edge, at the head of the stairs, fists upon his hips as he watched her. The paleness of him gleamed softly against the black, starred sky. One of his wings was hanging askew, she noticed suddenly, dangled awkwardly amid the rest. Aeriel remembered the darkangel's slow, limping retreat when last she had seen him, and realized he must have broken this pinion in the struggle with the Pendarlon.

The icarus did not fly now, but let her come. She was too far from him yet to see his face. She studied her feet as she mounted the slick, unrailed steps instead—one stair, two, twelve, twenty. She lost her count at thirty-seven.

Then abruptly, he stood before her. Aeriel halted on the last, top step; no more lay beyond. The vampyre blocked her path into the garden. She stood barely a pace from him, not looking at him. Her pulse was pounding from the long, steep climb.

The vampyre said, "So you have come back." Aeriel felt a dull surprise dart through her. His voice had lost its bell-like resonance. It sounded hollow now, grating. How ever could I have believed that voice beautiful? thought Aeriel. The vampyre demanded, "Why?"

Aeriel struggled to find her tongue. "I could not stay away," she managed at last—that was true enough—and found that though she was yet very afraid of him, she was no longer powerless to answer him.

He made a sound in his throat then that might have been acknowledgment, perhaps indifference or contempt. He said nothing for a moment, as if thinking, then drew breath suddenly. His words, when they came, sounded oddly agitated. "I knew you would return. All along I knew. That is why I did not bother to retrieve you from the Pendarlon when he so impudently snatched you from me." She watched his white, fisted fingers clenching and struggling against his palms. "I might have brought you back anytime I wished." His tone grew tighter, lighter, yet sounded at the same time strangely unsure. "But I knew you would be back soon or late. I let you return of your own, that you might see for yourself no one may defy me."

Aeriel said nothing. She could taste the falseness of his words. It was cowardice that had caused him to give her up to the Pendarlon—so much she was able to see even as she had lain wounded along her rescuer's back. Aeriel snorted, very softly, stared at the darkangel's feet: cowardice alone.

He said nothing more. She dared not glance up to see, but he seemed to be looking at her, studying her. Suddenly he put his hands upon her shoulders. Her knees went weak. "If you kill me now...," she started in a rush; her voice shook —but the words died on her lips when she raised her head to speak, and beheld the darkangel's face for the first time in many day-months.

Strangely, it had no power over her. His eyes were the same colorless crystal as before, his complexion white as ash; the leaden necklace still circled his throat. But he was no longer fair to look upon: across one cheek were the four long, bloodless slashes the Pendarlon had dealt him. They had not healed in all this time. The left shoulder of his garment hung in ribbons, and through the rips she saw the white, unbleeding wounds of his flesh.

He ignored her words, and she realized his gesture had not been intended as a threat. "You have grown, girl, since last I saw you." His tone was quieter now, almost curious. "You are no longer so bony. One may even tell you are a wench beneath that rag." The coldness of his palms numbed her shoulders. "And the sun," the vampyre mused, "has bleached your skin and hair. Perhaps the desert life agrees with you."

He slid his hands upward from her shoulders and Aeriel felt herself pale. Surely now he meant to strangle her—but he only placed his hands on either side of her face. Her cheeks stung with the chill.

"I had not known you had such eyes," the icarus was saying. "They are emerald. That is a rare color for eyes." He had called them fig-green once, thought Aeriel. The darkangel smiled, a coldly amused smile. "Do you know, I well believe you may be almost prettier now than was my last wife? She was a darksome thing, hair like black silk." Aeriel closed her eyes at the thought of Eoduin. "You were with her when I came upon her," the vampyre said. "Ah, how I thought you ugly then."

Aeriel opened her eyes and shuddered, looking at his torn face. The slashes of his cheek gapped and seamed shut when he spoke.

The vampyre grew uneasy beneath her gaze, shifted his stance. "What are you staring at?" he muttered.

Aeriel felt a sudden, inexplicable pity welling up in her, like that she had felt, when first she saw them, for the gargoyles and the wraiths. She did not realize she had reached to touch his wounds until she saw her hand upon his cheek. "Do they hurt you?" she asked him.

The vampyre dropped his icy hands from her face, pulled away from her and put his own fingers to the rends. "They burn," he snapped, half-turned from her. The quietness had left his voice. "But my mother will mend them. I shall go to her tomorrow morning, and she will sew them up with a silver thread." He glanced sidelong at Aeriel. "They will hardly show—the wing, too...."

"They will not heal of themselves?" began Aeriel, before she remembered that without blood, nothing heals.

The darkangel turned completely away. "No." His tone had soured. "It is a small price to pay for becoming an icarus. My mother will put it to rights. Besides, if I never heal, I also shall never scar." The feathers of his pinions ruffled, then smoothed into a dark cape as before. "My mother says I am far too handsome to be allowed to scar."

The one broken wing refused to settle. He stood fingering it. Aeriel could not see his face. She put her hand slowly to the scar on her own neck—a double crescent of colorless tissue—became aware in that same motion of the longer mark upon her forearm, now healed. They no longer pained her. It had never occurred to her to be ashamed of them. The Ma'a-mbai told tales around the cookfires of the winning of their scars. The icarus had begun to pace.

"By rights," he muttered, still fingering his injured pinion. His mood had darkened. "By rights I ought to kill you now, for having disobeyed me, run away, and dealt me these . . . very slight damages." He drew a long breath, evenly. "No less, they *have* proved troublesome." His fingers tightened on the wing. "And the dreams, though they have passed."

Aeriel almost drew back a step as his sharp gaze lanced across her—until she remembered that she stood upon the precipice, with no place to fall back upon but empty air.

The darkangel continued to eye her. "I could have killed you as you stood upon that mountain," he said harshly, "knife in hand—yet mercifully I spared you, brought you here." His white brow lowered dangerously above ice-colored eyes. "Yet thus and thus have you repaid me." He touched his wounded wing, the slashes as he spoke.

Aeriel gazed at him. And as he paced there,

under her gaze, there was no splendor to him anymore, no grace or majesty, only menace and vicious petulance. He has no power over me, she realized. A sixmonth ago I would have fallen at his feet. Her pulse had steadied since the climb. The warm wind from the plains was at her back. She held her ground beneath his glare.

"If you kill me now," she found herself saying then, in a voice that did not shake, "who will weave your last bride's wedding sari?" It was what she had faltered at saying before.

The vampyre stopped short. "A new bride," he murmured, "yes." Her words seemed to have diverted his attention. He dropped his wing. "I must take a new wife soon. This very month." He was no longer looking at Aeriel, gazed off across the garden. "And she shall be my final bride." The charms of his leaden necklace clinked as he nodded. "For a while, I shall go home and visit my mother then, and pay her just tribute. And when she has made me a true vampyre—" He smiled coldly; his voice grew velveted. "I shall join my six brothers, and we shall divide up the world between us."

The casualness of his assurance chilled her. Oh, he is evil, she told herself and longed to be away from him. "I must go and begin work at once," she told him, "if I am to complete the weaving of your bride's gown by nightfall."

The vampyre whirled, as if her unexpected words had made him suddenly aware of her again. She felt the wind of his whirling buffet her, was conscious how easily with one swift sweep of wing or arm he might bat her back over brink's edge to the plain far, far below. Watching him, his tightened lips and glaring eyes, for a moment she feared he might spring—but he subsided at last, breathing heavily. "Go, then," he said abruptly. "And weave."

Aeriel stood gazing at him, knowing she ought to be thankful, or surprised, and was neither— only relieved. "You will let me live." Now that he finally had granted it, she could think of nothing else to say.

"For now," he snapped. "Until the morrow." His voice sounded oddly hollow. "Before I leave this castle in the morning, I shall strangle you."

Aeriel faced him and said nothing, refusing to let her heart quail. If the vampyre were not dead by the morrow's morn, she told herself, her life would be worth little anyway.

The icarus turned from her, impatiently, made a gesture of dismissal. "Begone."

Aeriel left the top stone step, came forward into

the garden, started away from him through the wild-flowering, fruitless tangle. But as she went, she heard the rustle of wings as he turned again to view her.

"Ah, me," she heard him murmuring, "girl, even your walk has changed. You move straight-shouldered as a princess now, no longer creep and cringe like a little slave."

Aeriel fought an impulse to hunch, hurry away, hide from his gaze. She held to her pace and did not turn, for she feared that if she should so much as glance at him, he might call her back—and she did not trust his sudden quietness. It puzzled her. She could not make it out. He sighed then, as one might sigh over a lost trifle.

"It will be a pity killing you."

Aeriel gave no sign that she had heard. The softness of his words filled her with dread. She continued swiftly, steadily away from him across the garden, and took the steps down into the caves.

THE DUAROUGH WAS WAITING FOR HER AT the base of the stairs with a rushlight in his hand. Aeriel felt her heart lift now when she saw him. Her chill from the darkangel began to abate. She felt a smile dawning upon her lips, her first since she had left the Pendarlon. The little man gave a startled snort as he spotted her, fell back a pace.

"Heavens, but you've grown, child," he told her as she reached the bottom step, "and not all of that up."

Aeriel gave a laugh, and was surprised to find herself still capable of laughter. She brushed the tears from her cheeks. "I think perhaps that food laid into your magical pouch acquires magical properties, Little Mage of Downwending."

The duarough blushed and looked down at his feet. "So they still remember me by that name," he sighed, smiling. "I'll not deny I'm pleased."

Aeriel handed him the velvet pouch.

"The Avarclon's hoof," he asked, "the immortal one, mind you? Good, good." He took the pouch from her and put it in his sleeve. "I'm glad you figured out that much from the rime. If only I'd been given a little more time for explanations!" He glanced toward the ceiling, as though aware the darkangel stood in the garden above. Then he returned his gaze to Aeriel. "I must say, though," he exclaimed, "you took your own dear time about returning. I was half afraid you had given up or else run home."

Aeriel shook her head and felt the scar again. "The vampyre bit me. I was a long time healing."

At that the duarough blanched and held the rushlight high that he might see. He turned away, face drawn. "Daughter, daughter, I never meant that he should catch you. I sent word ahead...."

"The Pendarlon saved me," she said, "and left me with kind people until I grew strong."

The duarough sighed then, a little relieved. "Well, at least I know my magic has a bit of potence left. I was afraid the skiff would not transform, and then you would be left stranded without the lyon's knowing." He shook his head and clucked and put his fingers together. "I thought at first when you said the vampyre bit you, that you meant he had caught you and left you for dead. I knew that he had fought with the Pendarlon—his slashes and wing were proof of that—but I began to fear the leosol had come too late for the saving of you—you took such a time returning...."

He stopped himself, seemingly embarrassed at his own outpouring of words, and Aeriel laughed again.

"But enough of this." He clapped his hands with sudden vigor and became stern with himself. "For I have work to do, and so have you." He reached into the pouch and pulled the starhoof from it, stood gazing at it. "I must begin the brewing of the bridal cup, and you must make the gown." Then he halted again a moment, gazed earnestly at Aeriel, and his voice grew quieter, as though even yet he could not believe it. "Truly, daughter, are you well?" She nodded, and the duarough laughed, shaking his head. "Well, good, then. So I think we'd best be off, the both of us."

Then he hurried away down the shore along the river running. Aeriel felt a final, quiet laugh forming in her throat. He seemed a little in awe of her, and his sudden brusqueness was just to hide it. She turned and walked up the riverbank toward the steps that led up to the castle. Leaving the light and warmth of the caves, she felt the chill of the vampyre's keep descending upon her, but she shook it off. She had resolved herself in the garden above to have done with helpless dread. There was not time for it, and she had weaving to attend to.

WHEN AERIEL CAME TO THE ROOM OF THE wraiths, they were much as she had seen them when first she had come to the castle—they paced the floor, or sat rocking and moaning, or writhed and shrieked and tore their hair. They were all of them still thin as mummified birds: their starved faces held only dark, eyeless hollows, and their hair hung stiff and brittle as nettleseed silk. She still could tell none of them apart. The only difference was that the garments they wore were not the coarse, drab things she had seen them in at first, but light and airy shifts of spun charity.

The wraiths saw her standing in the doorway all at once, and some of them gave a feeble cry. She went into the room among them and they all gathered around and reached to touch her as though they could not believe she were really there. "You have come back," they said, "You have come back. You were gone a long time. We called for you and called," the lethargy of their voices telling Aeriel how pitifully their wits had dulled in her absence. "We grew so lonely with no one to talk to and sing us tales," they mumbled. Aeriel bit her lip, let out her breath and hoped she might, over the day-month's time, restore their faculties somewhat. "Why did you stay away so long?" pleaded the wraiths.

"I ran away from the castle," said Aeriel.

"But he has caught you again and returned you," they moaned.

She shook her head. "He caught me once, but at the last, I got away."

"But why did you return," they cried, rousing, "if you escaped him?"

Aeriel smiled. Already their reason seemed to

be quickening. "I only went because I had an errand to do. Now that is done, so I returned."

"But it is madness," cried the wraiths. "You were safe away from him. Why did you come back?"

"I promised I would help you," said Aeriel. "I could not leave you stranded here to die."

"We are grateful," said the wraiths, subsiding. They dropped their voices, glanced furtively about. "But you must hide. He will kill you if he finds you."

"He knows I am here," Aeriel replied, taking up her spindle from the floor where she had left it last. "And he means to kill me tomorrow." The wraiths began to moan again, but she soothed them, "Hush. Much may befall betwixt now and then."

She sat down on the low stool among the wraiths and began to spin. She was months out of practice, but she had not lost the knack: immediately a golden thread sprang to her fingers and she let the turning spindle drop. She had a host of new-learned desert tales to spin for them as well.

"Now," she said, "shall I tell you of my journey over the desert and under the plain?"

———

AERIEL SPENT MUCH OF HER TIME WITH the wraiths, spinning the thread for the garment of the vampyre's new bride and telling them stories of her sojourn on the desert and plain. She also went up to see the gargoyles often. At first they were as starved and as savage as before, but after she had fed them, they grew tame again, so docile in fact that though they still snapped and fought among themselves, some of them allowed her to caress them briefly, and a few would even take food from her hand.

She fell to studying the silver leashes that held them to the tower. And she saw that the chains were attached to each smooth brazen collar not by means of a lock, or even by a welded link, but rather by a slotted silver pin that might, by the proper sequence of sliding and turning, be slipped free. Nonetheless, though the weird beasts constantly tore at and worried their shackles, Aeriel perceived that only a human hand could trip the bolts and unloose their chains.

What time she did not spend with the wraiths and the gargoyles, she spent down in the caves with the duarough. He had converted the main treasury room into a sort of laboratory. A complex apparatus of slender metal tubes extended around the periphery with hardly a break, so that Aeriel could scarcely get in the door. Many dusty old books lay open about the floor, though in the middle of the room, there was still left considerable open space—and at the very center, the little fire burned as usual, unflagging and undying.

"Tell me," said Aeriel, sitting beside the fire, "how this will help us kill the vampyre."

The little man bustled about the apparatus. He hurried over to a book to consult some diagram or formula, then hurried back to adjust the flame under one of his bubbling containers. Then he brushed off his hands and came to sit by the fire with Aeriel.

"Out of this," he replied, gesturing at his handiwork, "I shall distill the bridal cup."

"You mean to poison him?" said Aeriel, quietly. Somehow, she had never before this brought herself to speculate what method they would use. It had not seemed real enough. But now the deed was imminent. Poison. So it was to be poison. It brought a bitterness into her mouth, knowing.

But the duarough was shaking his head. "Daughter," he chided, "the darkangel is poisoned already. This cup is no harm to any living creature, such as you or I, but to the vampyre, well..."

"What must I do?"

"You must give it to the bride to have him drink for a wedding toast. Do this when you attend her—by the way, how comes the spinning?"

"The spinning is done," said Aeriel, "and the weaving will be by late afternoon." She glanced over at the duarough's distillery. "And the icarus," she said, "I have not seen him lately. Where is he?"

The duarough rose and dusted his hands, turned back toward his apparatus. "He has flown," he answered. "He flew at noon to find a bride." The little man paused a moment, glanced back over his shoulder at Aeriel. "And you, daughter. How are you bearing up—still troubled dreams?"

She looked away, nodded. "Sometimes." Her sleep was never free of the darkangel now. Strange. When she had been beneath his spell, she had never dreamed of him. Aeriel rubbed her arms. "When the darkangel is dead," she murmured, more to herself than to the mage, "they will trouble me no more." She stood silent a moment, looking at nothing. Even now she could not shake off the cold. "It chills me to think what we are planning," she said.

Across from her, Talb sighed, turned back to adjusting his tubes and vials. "It chills me, too, betimes, daughter. But would you rather accept the alternative?"

Aeriel touched her throat and shook her head. "No. No." She rose and shoved the thought from her mind. If they did not slay the darkangel, their world would fall. She dropped her chafing arms and sighed. "Well, if, as you said, the vampyre is flown, I must go to them and set them free."

The duarough half-turned. "What's that?" he said. "What do you mean—the wraiths?"

Aeriel shook her head. "The gargoyles," she replied. "I resolved to free them as soon as he was gone."

The little man's brows drew together worriedly. "Daughter, he will not be much pleased with that, when he returns."

Aeriel sighed, and shook herself. "It makes no matter. To please him is no longer my great concern." She was a little surprised at the boldness of her words, even more surprised to find that they were true. "The gargoyles suffer. I shall free them."

The duarough looked at her then in very wonderment. "Five months of desert life," he said softly. "Ah, mistress, how you are changed."

TWELVE

Icarus' Bride

AERIEL FINISHED THE WEAVING BY LATE afternoon—a long piece of pale gold cloth finer and thinner and lighter than breath. And then she took the steps to the gargoyle tower. She knew they could hear her quiet step on the stairs because they had begun to give little moans and yips of anticipation at her approach. And when she emerged onto the circular terrace of the tower, the gargoyles descended from their platforms and strained toward her against their chains. She caressed each of them in turn: patting their rough reptilian hides, ruffling their fish-scales, or feathers, or fur.

"Run fast," she told them; "fly far, far off where he cannot find you if I fail."

Then she slipped the pins that held the chains to their collars (the collars themselves would not come free) and set the gargoyles at liberty. Those that could fly staggered into the air and coursed away in odd directions, more rapid than Aeriel would have thought possible on their skeletal wings. Those that could not plunged from the tower's top and landed, seemingly without injury, on the grassy plain far, far below. They streaked off in opposite directions, wailing a high, keening cry of freedom like great herons, or wild horses, or wolves.

Then Aeriel turned and descended into the castle again, to wait. Hours dragged and drifted by. The Planet waxed. Solstar sank lower in the ebon sky and the darkangel did not return. Aeriel fingered the cool step of the stone staircase on which she sat. The air of the stairwell chilled her, felt damp. Her palms prickled with sweat. Her mouth tasted of metal, zinc.

She found the wait interminable. She dared not seek out the duarough, lest she disturb his final preparations. And she did not believe that at the moment she could bear the company of the wraiths. Her one consolation was that as soon as the vampyre returned, she would have a companion. His final bride would join their plan, and then she, Aeriel, would not be so alone. She watched the sun decline through the wide casement by

which she sat, licked her dry lips, and whistled
Ma'a-mbai walking tunes softly to keep her courage up.

At last when the sun was low, barely an
hour from setting, the darkangel came, whirling
out of the west in a tangled fury of wings. Aeriel
sprang up and ran to the tower, but he was already coming down the steps when she arrived—
limping, favoring the foot he had burned in the
water of the caves many day-months past. Aeriel
stood on the inside steps of the tower, looking up
as he descended. His broken wing still hung
askew.

He spotted her but did not stop, came on toward her. His face was tight, his lips pressed thin.
He was alone. "There you are," he said shortly;
his tone was brittle. "I feared I might have to
search the keep for you. Is the weaving done?"

"Yes," she said, falling back a step for sheer
astonishment, "quite done. But..."

"But where is my bride?" he finished for her,
clenching and unclenching his fists as he came
down. "I could not find one—but no matter."
That last he growled. He swept past her on the
steps and continued down, still limping. Aeriel
hung back a moment, then followed. "That is not
to say there was not many a maid I could have

plucked away with ease," he snapped, "—but they were all so ugly. I think they are hiding the pretty ones from me." He ground his teeth. "I shall make them pay for that when I am made full icarus and rule. They shall give up their pretty ones to me in plenty then."

Aeriel stared after him, bewildered. She had never before heard such a torrent of words from him.

"But as it was," he continued, ill-tempered yet, but no longer raging, "there seemed to be no maidens much prettier than you, and as my wings were beginning to tire—the one being broken puts a strain upon the rest—I decided not to bother bringing one back, when I already had a maid here that would serve well enough...."

"What?" Aeriel exclaimed. She could not believe she had heard him right. What did he mean? She let out her breath suddenly—surely he could not mean her? Apprehension took her by the throat.

The vampyre continued, taking no notice that she did not call him "my lord" anymore. Indeed, he seemed almost mollified by her dismay. "You are not as pretty as some of my wives have been," he remarked, shrugging, "but you will do."

Aeriel halted on the steps and stared at him.

Her chest grew now so tight it hurt. "I don't understand," she heard herself saying. The echoes whispered back at her like bats' wings in the tower. She shook her head once, thought silently, desperately, no—surely he is but baiting me again.

The icarus snorted, glanced at her over his black, feathered shoulder. "Have I not made myself abundantly plain? You are to wear the bridal gown. Yes, you." He paused and stood a moment, half-turned, toying with his leaden chain. He gave her a mocking smile; she was not sure whether the mockery in it was meant for her or for himself. "Are you not honored?"

Aeriel stood dumb.

He eyed her and then nodded, to himself, as though the prospect of wiving her did not displease him as much as he had thought. "Go prepare yourself," he told her, "and I shall do the same. You know where my chambers are. I shall leave them unlocked. Be there, just at sunset, and I shall come to you."

Aeriel said nothing, nor moved.

"By the way," he remarked, almost casually. Her horror seemed to have restored his humor. "Where are my gargoyles? They are not up above."

Aeriel nodded. It was a long moment before she could speak. "I know. I set them free."

The icarus turned on her suddenly. "Freed them?" he spat. All trace of amusement washed from him. His ice eyes flashed. For the second time since her return Aeriel feared he might forget his word, spring upon her there and throttle her. But he restrained himself, barely. His cold, white eyes never left her face. "No matter," he murmured. His breath was harsh. "I shall need no more watchdogs after tonight." He fiddled with the chain about his neck. "It is well you are to be my wife, girl," he breathed thickly, "or I should be displeased."

Abruptly he swung away from Aeriel, put his back to her and started once more down the turning stair. His black wings rustled like stormwind through high grass. Reaching the bottom step, he swept out of the tower with never a backward glance. Aeriel felt dizzy. She sat down upon the deserted stair. Her heart was beating very hard in the tightness of her throat. She could not think. She had expected an ally—no more than a frightened girl, perhaps, but some helpmate. Thought of the task ahead almost overwhelmed her. Now it fell upon her alone.

She felt crushed, breathless, but she made herself take breath. Her knees were weak, but she forced herself to rise. The duarough was waiting for her. The wraiths depended on her. And her own life hung on this now as well. A kind of calm stole over her, more numbness, she thought dimly, than calm. Slowly, she went down the stairs. Going out into the garden then, she followed the long steps into the caves.

THE DUAROUGH WAS IN THE TREASURE room at his apparatus as she had expected him to be. He held a strangely shaped metal bowl in his hand under a glass tube that dripped, slowly dripped a clear, glowing liquid into the bowl. He glanced over his shoulder when Aeriel came in, but did not turn around.

"Has the icarus returned?"

Aeriel did not answer him at first, stood silent for a time. Then she said faintly, "Yes."

The little man murmured his acknowledgment and adjusted some coupling of his apparatus with one hand. "And you have spoken with his bride?"

Still he did not turn.

Aeriel drew breath. "I did not have to," she told him, "for it is I."

The duarough started and nearly spilled the liquid he was catching. The cup was brimful. He reached and turned the key in the side of the glass tubing; the liquid ceased to drip. He put the bowl down beside him on the stack of books. A single drop slipped over the edge. She saw the little gobbet of bright liquid disappear in a puff of vapor the instant it left the rim of the bowl—and Aeriel realized then that it was not a bowl at all, but the hoof of the equustel.

"Now will you tell me," she asked him, "how we shall kill the vampyre?"

The duarough stood facing her, his back pressed to the distillery. His small stone-colored eyes had widened. "Daughter," he murmured, "what did you say?"

"Tell me," began Aeriel, flatly, "how shall we ... ?" but the little man's sputtering cut her off.

"Before that."

Aeriel looked away. "It is I," she repeated softly. "The vampyre has chosen me for his bride. There is no other."

The duarough let out his breath then, seemed to sag. "Ye gods," he breathed, "O Ancient Ones. What shall be done?" But in a moment he regained himself. His eyes flicked back to hers. "Aeriel," he said. "I am afraid for you. If you should fail ..."

"I shall die," she heard herself saying; her voice

sounded oddly dispassionate, "forever, as will my friend Eoduin, and all the others of the wraiths. Then the seven icari will be made invincible, and they will rule the world."

She felt her scattered thoughts beginning to return now, after the shock of learning she was the icarus' bride. She was more clearly aware of the chamber around her, could feel her own body more distinctly. She remembered a desert proverb suddenly, one she had learned from Orroto-to: "Go coward into battle, and you will fall. Go brave, and you may not. And if not heart-brave, at least face-brave." Aeriel put on the bravest face she could, then, and turned back toward the duar-ough.

"But I do not intend to fail." Her voice held more assurance than she felt. "Now tell me what to do."

The little man stood looking at her a moment, chewing one knuckle, his eyes deep with concern. Then he took hold of himself as well, murmured, "Ah, well, if we must, we must." He crossed the room to where the fire burned. "So little time," he fidgeted. "So little time."

Then he fell on his knees by the flickering wreath of white flame. All the floor was pale lime-stone, but the pits had been filled with smooth white sand. The fire had been built over one of these, Aeriel saw, as the duarough began to dig in the soft grit. The brushwood, dislodged from its stack, fell over and smothered out as the little man dug determinedly with his hands, tossing the pale grains, careless of where they fell.

Aeriel drew breath as the flames died and darkness leapt to fill the room. "Why have you done that?" she whispered at him. The sudden dark uneased her.

But then she saw that the room was not quite all dark. Tiny flames beneath the glass vessels still burned—too faint to relieve the gloom, but there was another light in the chamber. On the floor, at the very center where the duarough dug, the sand glowed—or rather, she saw, it was not the sand but something beneath the sand, shining up through the translucent grains.

"Patience, daughter," the duarough said. "We'll not need that little fire in just a moment."

He brushed the last of the sand away from the object in the small pit he had made. Its light shone forth and filled the room. It was a dagger with a blade like a snaking ray of the sun. The duarough lifted it reverently, and Aeriel saw the fine chain falling from its haft.

"What is it?" she murmured, staring. The darkness and the duarough's solemnity caused her to hush her voice.

"The edge adamantine," he answered, proudly. "It fell into my keeping—oh, a long time past." He held the dagger out to her. Aeriel drew back, surprised. "Take it with you," he explained, "when you go to the vampyre's chambers. I cannot follow until the sun is down. Keep it concealed if things go aright. But if things fall awry, draw it out: its light will blind him and its heat scathe him until you may escape."

Aeriel looked at the blade that burned like starfire, reached to take it from him and put the chain about her neck; beneath her garment, the blade fell against her breastbone, lay close against her between her breasts. She fingered its haft. The duarough rose and moved off a moment, then returned and put the hoof of the starhorse into her hands. Its contents shone.

"Only the chalice-hoof of the immortal horse can hold this liquor," he informed her.

"What is it?" Aeriel inquired.

He shook his head. "Fear not to drink of it yourself, daughter. Its properties are marvelous, and it is bane only to the vampyre and his kind."

Aeriel arose. "I must go," she told the duarough, "and prepare." The two means the little mage had put into her hands had steadied her. She cradled the chalice-hoof in cupped palms, careful not to spill any.

The duarough laid his hand on hers a moment. "Yes, child," he answered, "go. There is not time to lose."

AERIEL STOOD IN THE SPINNING ROOM amid the wraiths. She knew the sun was nearly down, despite her haste to bathe her body in the warm, bright water of the cave, to comb her now electrum-pale hair, to wind about her the yards and yards of sari into a bridal gown. But among the wraiths she stood now, attired as the vampyre's bride.

She said, "The time has come. I am going to slay the darkangel now, and rescue your souls." For all the bravery of the words, she could not quite keep the tremor from her voice.

"But why do you go," one of the wraiths said, "attired as a bride?" Their minds had slowly come back to them, trace by trace, over the last daymonth.

"Because he means to take me as his bride," said Aeriel.

The wraiths moaned and muttered. "So this is how he punishes you for running away."

A shaky laugh escaped Aeriel. She let it go, as much to relieve her tension as express her irony. "No. He thinks to honor me."

"As he has honored us," they shrieked. "He has honored us to death."

"Hush, hush," cried Aeriel. "I will not let him kill me. I have the chalice that will lay him low, and the blade to breach his heart."

The wraiths murmured dolefully. "We fear for you," they said. "Let us come with you. We are so thin, we may hide anywhere—in the curtains, in the bedclothes with never a wrinkle. We are not strong, but we are horrible to look at. He pretends only contempt for us, but we know we frighten him." The wasted women nodded eagerly, then consulted among themselves. "If you should falter," one of them said to Aeriel, "or things should run amiss, we might be of use to you."

She started to protest, and would have bid them stay, save that they wept and wailed and clung to her so, Aeriel knew they would not let her go until she agreed. Reluctantly, she resigned herself. And despite herself, she was glad of companions—anyone to accompany her now. She nodded.

"Follow me, then," she bade the wraiths, and

their delighted laughter sounded like sand scritching softly over a dry stone floor.

The nearest wraith took hold, in her frail, mummy-like hands, of the hem of Aeriel's garment. The next wraith took hold of her sister's hem, and those behind did the same until they formed a train. Seizing the chalice firmly in both hands, Aeriel led them out of their chamber and into the hall.

The white, soft setting glare of Solstar shone long veils through the windows. The broad interstices of shade in between were empty black. Passing now from light to dark to light again, Aeriel found herself sweating and shivering by turns. She tried to hold the bright bowl steady.

Glancing back over her shoulder, she eyed the crumpled train of wraiths. They were so bent and fragile now, and most of them so nearly blind, they would have lost their way at once in the rambling corridors without her guidance. So thin were they, they seemed translucent. Aeriel could scarcely see them in the waning brightness, lost them completely in the velvet shadows.

Their progress seemed maddeningly slow. Solstar was already half sunk away. Aeriel balanced the brimming cup and urged the feeble wraiths forward. They made what haste they could. At last they reached the vampyre's quarters, set at the end of the long, empty hall. Aeriel felt all her impatience evaporating into dread.

Slowly, she led the wraiths up the long, straight stair to the small, ornately fashioned door. It stood fast shut—she had never seen it open—but when she lifted the latch, it gave inward, swung open. Aeriel hesitated a long moment, then led the wraiths inside.

The outer chambers were spacious and, to her great surprise after living so long in the vast, deserted keep, fully furnished with stools and tables, cushions, curtains, cabinets, and shelves. She and the wraiths passed through or beside sitting rooms, servants' quarters, a tiled bath, a study. Aeriel found herself admiring the mosaic inlay of subtle-hued soapstone and the pillars of smooth, colored marble.

They came to the suite's inner chamber last, and it seemed very small in comparison. Long curtains fell beside columns partitioning the room proper from the broad outside terrace. The bed was small, but carved of some dark, rare wood, and richly canopied.

At the foot of the bed lay a chest such as one might store clothes or linens in, but as she drew near to it, Aeriel saw it must be a toychest, for on its inlaid lid rested two playthings only a princeling might have: a dragon carved of ivory, with claws of black onyx, and a rag doll of costly satins and velvets, sewn with pearls.

As she set the chalice down beside the playthings on the chest, it occurred to Aeriel that this must have been a child's room before the dark-angel came. It puzzled her that nothing in the room had been disturbed, nothing taken by the queen and her people, when they had removed to Esternesse.

The dusk-lit room went suddenly dark. Aeriel started, turned, realized even as she did so that it was only Solstar having set. She went to turn up the oil lamps that burned low in niches in the walls. The wraiths milling about the room turned their blind eyes from the light. As Aeriel brightened the final lamp, one of the wasted women halted.

"He is coming!" hissed the wraith.

The others stopped. Aeriel stopped. She dropped her hand from the lamp, padded swiftly to the center of the room. She stood, arms folded across her breast, listening. The silence of the great deserted keep strained against her ears. Then above the soft hissing of the lampwicks' burning, she caught sound of something: uneven footfalls moving across the great hall outside, the rustle of many wings.

"Quick." Aeriel gestured to the wraiths, her voice a tight whisper, lest he hear. "Hide yourselves."

The starved women melted into the shadows and the dim places of the room, became motionless, invisible. Aeriel lifted the horse's hoof and held it cupped in her hands.

The footsteps drew nearer across the hall. She heard the darkangel ascending the long, straight stair, crossing through the outer chambers. Aeriel tried to steady her trembling hands. She stood facing the doorway. The soft white lamplight played pale shadows across the walls. The vampyre's halt step stalked nearer, nearer. Aeriel closed her eyes and held her breath.

The footfalls ceased. Aeriel opened her eyes. The icarus stood in the doorway before her. His deep black pinions, save for the one, fell like a mantle from his shoulders. His colorless eyes looked her up and down, once.

"Well, wife," he said. The long rends in his face and shoulder gaped. "You are very beautiful, almost worthy of me." Aeriel drew a long, shuddering breath at the sight of him. The vampyre smiled. "You tremble—are you cold? Soon you will not mind the cold."

He left the doorway and came toward her. Aeriel clutched the silver hoof.

"What is that?" he said.

Aeriel glanced at the vessel in her hand. She spoke and tried to keep her voice steady. "It is the custom of my people to drink a bridal cup."

He laughed. "A quaint custom. I had not heard of it." He settled back, arms folded, eyeing the cup in her hands. "But we are not among your people now."

Aeriel gazed at him, felt her blood quicken. "But," she stammered, "you must drink."

"And why is that?" the vampyre inquired.

Fear welled up to drown her thoughts. She searched desperately for some persuasion, felt the blade of the hidden dagger burning upon her breast. "It would please me," she began, "for you to drink...."

The icarus' arms unfolded. His hands went to his hips. "And why should I suffer to do anything at all that pleases you?" he scoffed, sharp-edged annoyance creeping into his voice. "I am the master here."

A notion surfaced; Aeriel let out her breath.

Her blood returned. A lump of relief rose in her throat. She schooled her voice to be forceful and clear. "If you do not drink, husband-to-be, we will not be truly wed. Then you will have not fourteen brides, but only twelve-and-one." The vampyre snorted, pursed his lips in scorn. "Come, it is a small concession," she pressed. "Why quibble?"

The icarus dropped his hands from his hips suddenly and laughed, a dark and irritated laugh. "Very well," he snapped. "Let us drink, wench, since you are so adamant. I will have my own way in all things soon enough." He held out his hand. "Give me the cup."

But Aeriel had already raised the vessel to her own lips. The dram smelled faintly of almond milk. She sipped; the drink was warmer than liquor and cooler than mint, the taste strong and bittersweet, like hornflowers, but much deeper. Its warmth spread through her body. She felt suddenly stronger, more awake and more alive. The lamps about the chamber seemed to burn brighter against the dark. She held out the hoof of the starhorse to the icarus. He took it in his hand and laughed again.

"A curious vessel," he remarked, frowning. "It reminds me of...of..."

Aeriel felt her veins constrict. She knew she

must say something, lest he grow wary. "We...
we borrowed the tradition from the plains."

The vampyre shrugged, ignoring her. "I cannot
think what," he finished, raised the silver hoof to
his lips and downed its contents in a draught.
Aeriel watched him, and dared not breathe. He
smiled at her and laid the cup aside.

"Now we are wed," he said. "What was the
dram—wine of some tree you found fruiting in
the garden?"

Aeriel shook her head. "Nothing fruits in your
garden."

"Oh?" he said, not greatly interested. His eyes
devoured her. "What was it, then?"

"I don't know," said Aeriel. Unease crouched
between her shoulder blades. Why did he not
fall?—did he not feel the liquor's heat? She had
felt its burning warmth at once, still felt it. Aeriel
fell back a step as the darkangel advanced.

He stopped, seemingly amused at her retreat.
"What do you mean?" he asked, toying with the
leaden vials at his throat. Aeriel eyed his lean,
white fingers, imagined their strength: fingers that
snapped bats' bones and tore out lizards' tongues,
throttled his brides to death that he might drink
off their blood, steal away their souls, and tear out
their hearts for the gargoyles. Aeriel felt faint.

"Surely it was some fruit of my garden," he said.

She held him off with her eyes, felt herself growing desperate. He was no weaker—seemed if anything stronger than before. A slow panic crept over her. The duarough had been mistaken. The darkangel was invincible. No poison could touch him. He was frowning slightly now, since she did not answer.

"The duarough gave it to me," she said; she could not think of any lie.

The vampyre looked at her, uncomprehending. "Who—?" he started, but stopped short. His skin, always before so translucent fair, went suddenly waxy. He laid a hand on his throat and swallowed hard. His wings, no longer folded, poised tensely, like a dozen hawks ready to stoop. His frown deepened; his lips tightened into a grimace. Then he wrapped his arms about his middle with a cry.

"Poison. You have poisoned me—ah! I burn!"

He sank down on one knee, his face twisted in pain. Aeriel shrank back from him, appalled. She had not known it would be like this. The duarough had never told her the potion would bring him pain. She had imagined he would fall insensate at the first sip. The darkangel's head jerked up; the leaden necklace clinked, and she saw his eyes—wild and bright.

"After the great honor I have done you," he cried hoarsely, "choosing you first as my servant, now as my wife—this is your repayment?"

He gasped and twisted, clutching his waist. His face contorted as in agony. Aeriel pressed her hands over her mouth to keep from screaming.

"I am on fire," he said through clenched teeth, panting with the effort. "You have killed me— but you'll not live to celebrate it."

He struggled to his feet, his dark wings thrashing wildly. Their wind stirred the gauze hangings, flattened her sari's folds against her body, made the oil lamps gutter. But for all their desperate fury, they could scarcely help him rise. He clutched at the bed-curtain, reached out his free hand toward Aeriel, leaned forward to enfold her in his wings.

She shrank away from him, threw up her arm to keep him away. One cold-biting hand of the icarus closed over her wrist. Aeriel heard herself scream as he dragged her toward him. She snatched at the dagger hidden in her gown, but before she could draw it, the wraiths appeared.

Swiftly, silently, they fleeted from the shadows, the folds of the bed-curtains, the seams of the walls. The icarus' hand went suddenly limp; Aeriel saw him start. She slipped free of him as the wraiths surrounded him, stood ringed about him, keeping him from Aeriel. The vampyre cried out at the sight of them, threw up his arms as if to ward them away.

"What are you doing here, my wives?" he cried. "You are so hideous to look at. Keep off!"

The wraiths drifted in a slow circle around him. "We will not keep off," they said. "You have chosen us, and we are yours."

"Why are you so ugly?" he wailed. "Why do you torment me? Why are all my wives so ugly?" His strength was slipping from him now. His wings ceased their buffeting. He sank slowly to his knees.

"Stolen our souls," said the wasted women. "What could we have become but hideous?"

"Drunk off our blood," another one said, "but left us just wit enough to suffer in our fate— horrible suffering."

"Traitors," the icarus gasped. "I favored you above all others."

"Torn out our hearts," the wraith-women hissed. "See what your 'favor' has brought us to. Liar."

"Pillager."

"Murderer."

"Thief."

The vampyre leaned upon one hand now. The other one clutched his side. As he stared at the faces of the withered creatures stepping slowly past him, Aeriel saw a last gleam of defiance light his eye. "What does it matter?" he whispered, his breath faint and harsh. "What could any of your worthless lives matter? I am the darkangel, a thousand thousand times above you. I shall rule this world—" His ranting whisper weakened further. "My mother has promised me..."

"Never," answered his wives, and silenced him.

The vampyre sagged, slumped forward to the floor. Aeriel watched through the circling wraiths. If he protested still, she could no longer hear him. He struggled feebly for a moment on his side, then with a jerk, rolled over onto his back. His wings crumpled beneath him. His rigid frame relaxed. Aeriel found herself clutching her own throat as his gasps grew fainter. His head turned from side to side, and was still. His colorless eyes closed slowly, opened. He heaved a deep, shuddering sigh. His eyelids slid shut then and did not open again.

He was breathing only very lightly now. He was not dead. Aeriel felt all of her energy draining from her. She sank down very slowly and leaned back against the cold, wet stone of the wall. The blade adamant lay hot and sharp against her beneath the fabric of her gown. She felt the fine metal chain pressing into her neck. She did not look at the fallen darkangel. She did not want to see him. Aeriel closed her eyes for a long moment to rest.

THIRTEEN

Change of Heart

~~~

WHEN AERIEL OPENED HER EYES, ALL WAS
as it had been a few moments before. The icarus
lay pale and still on his crumpled black wings. The
thirteen wraiths stood wan and motionless around
him. Aeriel arose at last and walked past them to
the vampyre. She knelt beside him and unfastened
the necklace from his throat.

His flesh was colorless and cold as death. Her
hands were shaking. At first she feared to see him
rot and fall to ashes at her touch, but he breathed
on. And then she fully expected him to awake
from feigned sleep and strangle her, but he did not
stir. She lifted the leaden chain in her hand and
unhooked the first vial from its link.

She turned and held it up. "Whose soul is
this?" she asked.

One of the wraiths came forward—perhaps the

most bent and wasted of them. "It is mine," she said, her voice so thin it sounded like little more than wind. "You must help me."

The wraith's emaciated fingers closed about Aeriel's hand. She helped the creature raise the leaden vessel to her lipless mouth and drink. For such a tiny vial, it seemed she drank a very long time. When she was done, the wraith stepped back, but she was no longer a wraith. She now had eyes where only hollows had been, and though her body was as starved and fleshless as before, there was now an energy about it, almost a glow.

"My name is Marrea," said the creature who no longer was a wraith. Her voice was soft and full, very beautiful. "I was a daughter of a goose-herd in the forested hills of Bern. I was tending my flocks in the meadows one morning when the darkangel seized me."

Then before she had quite spoken the last of it, her body fell away into dust; her bones crumbled and settled in a heap—yet still she stood there before Aeriel. Or rather, it was another being that stood in her place, a being made of a soft yellow light that retained a human shape. The shift Aeriel had woven for her draped softly about her, but the outline of her form shone faintly through. She looked to Aeriel like a beautiful young woman.

"See me as I was before," the spirit said. "Now that you have given me back my soul, I have no more use for my body. My heart and my lifeblood are gone irreplaceably: I am no longer of this world, so I must leave body behind. But this"— she touched her kirtle—"which you have given me, I will retain, for love is immortal, and eternal, and will not wither in the endless deeps of heaven."

The spirit rose. Her image grew thinner, more transparent, and her soft light diffused. She ascended more swiftly as Aeriel watched. Her garment rippled gently in some wind that Aeriel could not feel. The spirit receded to the upper reaches of the night sky. Her light grew smaller and farther away until it seemed no more than a fallow star in a dark swatch of the heavens where no other stars burned.

Aeriel gazed at the now-motionless point of light a long moment before she could bring herself back to the task at hand. The other wraiths already were moaning and clamoring for their souls. Aeriel gave out the vials one by one, then watched as one by one the mummy-women drank, and their bodies fell away, leaving only the bright images of their souls. And in turn each told her name, and where she was from, and what she had been in life, and how the vampyre had taken her. Slowly, they ascended.

Then Aeriel gave to the last wraith the last vial but one. And when the creature drank, and her body fell to dust, Aeriel recognized the spirit's features, though they were made of golden light. "Eoduin," she cried softly. "Eoduin."

"Yes, companion," the spirit said; her voice was lovely, bell-like in tone, but still recognizably Eoduin's. "You were my servant once, and I was careless of you, even as I was jealous of your fortitude."

"I have no fortitude," Aeriel whispered.

The golden maiden smiled. "When the icarus took me, did you not go to avenge me? As a friend would have done, and not a slave."

"I was desperate," she protested softly. "I was in despair. Your father would have sold me...."

But the other spoke on, still smiling. "And when you found me among those others, a wretched, mindless wraith, still you came to us, though we were hideous to look at. You did not know which one I was, and so you loved us all for my sake. Now you have felled the icarus and returned to us our souls. Thirteen stars will burn bright in heaven for you, Aeriel."

So saying, she rose into the sky. Looking up, Aeriel saw fixed stars in the patch of heavens that had formerly been dark. As she watched, that last of the spirits joined the constellation: a perfect, tilted circle like a crown, or maidens dancing—save that one spot was empty. That will be my place, thought Aeriel, when I depart the world. She looked down at the last, empty vial on the leaden chain. And there my soul would have rested, had I let the vampyre take me.

She laid the heavy chain down and gazed at the unconscious darkangel. He lay absolutely still, save for his quiet, shallow breaths. Helpless now, and unaware, he looked more pathetic than terrible, more wasted than ugly. Aeriel touched the unbleeding and unhealing slashes on his shoulder and cheek. The awful coldness of his flesh numbed her fingertips.

A great white light filled the darkened chamber. Aeriel spun around. The duarough stood in the doorway with a torch of rushlight in his hand. Aeriel wondered how long it had been since sundown—no more than half an hour surely—only the time it had taken the duarough to make his way up from the caverns and through the long, twisting halls of the castle to this room. The little man was puffing and blowing when he entered, so she knew he must have hurried. Aeriel wondered that she had not heard him coming.

"Ah, daughter," he panted, "I see you are quite well, so perhaps there was not need for all the haste I made. I"—he had to pause for breath—"I heard a scream."

Aeriel turned her face away, touched her wrist. "He caught hold of me," she murmured. "But the wraiths saved me."

"The wraiths?" the little mage mused. "So they proved to be of use at last—and you did not need the dagger after all." He puffed a sigh, folded his hands, nodded. "Well, I am glad."

Aeriel glanced back at him. "Your poison has done its work," she said, surprising herself with the stiffness of her tone. "What was it?"

"Poison?" snorted the duarough as he seated himself. "Daughter, it was hardly that. It was life, health, warmth—call it what you will. It is in all plants, in the nectar of hornflowers, in animals: it is the dram that flows from the wellspring of Aiderlan, and infuses all the waters of the world. Even in the Dead Lake of the lorelei there is a little of the water of life, elsewise that mere would be truly dead, devoid even of her nearly dead creatures. Even she is yet a little alive." He indicated the fallen icarus. "As is he. But he is mostly dead, and it is the deadness in him that rejects the vigor of that dram."

The duarough took a quiet survey of the room before eyeing the little heaps of ashes on the floor.

"Well," he said, "I see you've done with the vampyre's wives. I must say, I'm glad to see the last of that lot. All that wailing and moaning—one could scarcely think...."

"Here is the knife," said Aeriel. She drew it out from beneath her bridal gown and lifted the chain from around her neck. She had spoken more to quiet him than from need, for he could plainly see it, shining brighter than his torch.

The duarough's manner was the same as always—brisk and talkative—but just now it grated on her terribly. It seemed an abomination for him to run on so lightly in face of the deed they were about to do. And she knew full well that they must kill the icarus. A season past, on the steeps of Terrain, she had relished the thought, but now it sickened her, for she no longer feared him, nor loathed him, nor worshipped him as she had done before.

She felt a curious kind of pity for him now, a pity for his present helplessness, and an almost-longing for his former might. He had been terrible and evil, yes, but also very beautiful. Now they were going to destroy him—as he had meant to destroy the wraiths, this world, and her, Aeriel reminded herself. Yet the memory of his beauty haunted her, and she felt suddenly overwhelmed with a sorrow she did not entirely understand.

Aeriel held out the knife to the mage. "You do it," she told him. "I cannot."

The duarough rose and came over to her, eyed her quizzically. "Daughter," he said, "only the children of the upperlands-under-the-sky can wield that blade and strike true. It was not made for the hand of a son of earth."

"Of course," said Aeriel, softly. "I should have known."

Bitterness and misery mixed with the pity in her breast as she took the dagger more firmly in her grasp. It seemed to have no weight at all. She closed both hands around its haft, glanced from the fallen icarus to her companion.

"Give me some word to bolster me in this," she begged him.

"Plunge the blade into his heart," the duarough said, "and it is done."

There was no rancor in his voice, no malice at all. Nonetheless, she was filled with disgust at his words and at herself, for she knew she must obey them. She gazed down at the darkangel; he lay there yet, as still as death—and yet, she knew he lived. She raised the blade above his breast and tried to close her eyes.

She knew she could have done it, had only she shut her eyes—shut out the light of the lamps, and stars, and the duarough's torch, and blade—saying, "For Eoduin," or "This is not killing; he is already dead," or "This is not the darkangel; it is someone I do not know." But she could neither close her eyes, nor speak, nor move. She held the dagger bright above him for a very long time before she lowered it slowly and laid it on the floor.

"I cannot," she said. "I cannot kill him."

"But you must," the duarough admonished gently, tentatively, almost as if he were testing her.

"There is nothing that I *must* do," snapped Aeriel, more fiercely than she meant. She made her voice a little quieter, but no less firm. "I am free to make this choice, and I choose he shall not die."

They sat in silence for a very great while. She could not turn to face him, but she knew he was looking at her, studying her. She knew that he had trusted her, depended on her to do this thing. She had even convinced herself that it might be possible after all, only to discover now, at this last moment, that she could not. She had failed the mage and herself. One warm tear slid down her cheek and yet she felt, strangely, no great sorrow.

"What, then, do you propose to do with him?" the little man inquired.

"I..." Aeriel drew breath and was surprised to find it ragged. "I do not know. I want..." She was trying to say something, she knew, but was not even sure herself quite what it was.

"Tell me what you want," her companion said.

Aeriel bit her lip and touched the fallen icarus' face. The icy chill of his cheek numbed her hand and she did not care. "The lorelei has drunk his blood, hardened his heart," she answered softly. "He is as much her prisoner as the wraiths were his. As I pitied them once, must I not pity him now? My heart..." Her breaths were coming so short now she had to pause. "My heart goes out to him. I want..." She stumbled, sat a moment, silent. "I wish that I might save him from the witch as I have saved the wraiths from him."

She turned to face the duarough now and to her surprise found him eyeing her with the barest trace of smile on his lips. She feared he was mocking her.

"He is monstrous and evil," she cried, despairing; "I know it well. But his soul is still his own —there is that final spark of good in him." Her throat felt tighter than she had ever known. She dropped her eyes. "He is not quite a vampyre yet."

The little mage laughed softly then, and Aeriel realized it was not mockery, but approval lit his eye. "It is that spark, then, daughter," he said, "that you must seize and kindle, if you are to save him."

Aeriel looked up at him. "What do you mean?" she said.

"The icari are made, not born," the duarough replied. "He was not always this way. He was a child of mortals once...."

"You mean the witch's doing may be undone?" cried Aeriel. "He might become a man again?" The prospect astonished her. She had feared it all vain hope and dreaming.

The magician nodded judiciously. "Perhaps," he told her, "and perhaps."

She felt a surge of anger in her breast. "Why did you not tell me this before?" she heard herself demanding. "I might have killed him needlessly."

The duarough shook his head, smiling. "No, child. I do not think there was ever any danger of that. And I did not tell you before because nothing could have come of it. To heal requires true love, and you did not love him before, though now I see you are beginning to."

Aeriel stared at the mage and her anger cooled, slowly, into astonishment. How could he say she loved the vampyre? The thought had never occurred to her. Then it began to dawn in her mind, slow as sunrise, that perhaps she did in some ways love him. She admired the beauty, the magnificence, the grace and power that had once been his. But if this were love, it was not blind, for she still abhorred his cruelty, his cowardice, his impatient and imperious self-interest.

She gazed at the duarough and said, "Yes. I think that I do love him in a way, and I do not want him to perish." She turned to look down at the fallen darkangel now. "I want to save him. Tell me how."

But the little mage of Downwending said, "I cannot. My magic has no province here. The cure must come from you."

Aeriel gazed at him, uncomprehending. "I have skill at neither medicine nor magic," she said.

"It is not required," the duarough told her. "Think, child; think what ails him!"

Aeriel looked down at the pale face of the vampyre. "He has no blood," she said. "The water witch has drunk it all. He cannot live again as a mortal without blood."

"Then you must find him some," the magician said.

"But the only living blood in the world," insisted Aeriel, "flows in the veins of living creatures. I cannot kill one to save another."

"True," the duarough replied.

"Then it is hopeless," cried Aeriel, filled with rage at her own helplessness and the injustice of this pass. Her eyes burned with tears.

"Cup your hands and catch the tears," the mage instructed. He reached to bring her hands together in a bowl, and even as he spoke the falling tears turned to blood that welled up and filled her hands in a moment.

"But I thought you said your magic...," Aeriel whispered, staring.

"Oh, this is not my doing," the duarough said. "Greater magics than mine are afoot in this chamber, where blade and cup and dram are met with love such as yours. All lies in your hands now, daughter. I am no more than your aide."

Aeriel stared at the living blood brimming her cupped hands, and then at the darkangel. "But this will not be enough," she said. "It cannot be."

"It will suffice," the duarough said. "As one drop of your charity spins endless thread, so one tear of your true love will make enough for this." Then he tilted her hands so that the blood fell in a thin stream to the vampyre's white breast, and there disappeared like rain into a thirsty earth. Aeriel poured for a long, long time before her hands were empty of blood. By that time, color had come into the vampyre's skin. He was no longer deathly white. No spot or stain was left upon his breast, and Aeriel's hands were as clean and dry as before. She watched as traces of blood arose to fill the slashes on his face and shoulder.

She gazed at the duarough in wonderment. "You are a wizard," she told him, "and a great one."

But again the duarough shook his head. "I have done nothing, child," he told her. "Nor could I, had I tried. Mages cannot work everything. Only the quality of your mercy could have accomplished—" He cut himself off abruptly, then, with a glance at the darkangel. "But haste," the little man cried, "or he dies. You have given him his lifeblood back, but his heart is still lead. The dram he drank will sustain him for a little, but not long."

She caught in her own breath sharply as she realized that already the icarus' breaths were fading.

"What must I do?" said Aeriel, but the duarough did not reply. The moment she sat gazing at him seemed to last many heartbeats, though she knew in truth it spanned but two. Then she resolved herself and spoke. "The cure must come from me, you said. Very well; I have not come this far only to see him die. He must have a heart of flesh to live, and if it must be mine, I'll freely give it."

She did not look at the duarough again, to see if he would try to stay her. Giving him no time to intercede, or even speak, she reached for the dagger. Quickly, but very carefully, she drew the bright blade down the vampyre's breast—so keen was its edge that no blood sprang to the wound. His flesh parted, and amid the folds she found his heart—a cold, hard, dreary lump of lead.

She lifted it out and set it down, a dry, bloodless, heavy metal weight, then took up the blade again and turned it to her own breast. The shining blade was so keen she felt no sting, only heat like the light of Solstar. Lifting her own heart from her breast, she felt only emptiness remain. She laid her heart of flesh within his open breast, then folded his flesh over again, where it joined without a seam.

She felt tired, very spent—yet at the same time, there was a curious lightness to her limbs. The colors of the room faded. She could not seem to keep her eyes open. Her breaths were growing short and shallow. It felt like the coming on of sleep, this dying. She sank down onto the floor, laid her head down on her arm, and closed her eyes.

FOURTEEN

Awakening

~❧

THE DUAROUGH STOOD TRANSFIXED WITH wonder and astonishment, watching Aeriel as she cut out the lump of lead from the darkangel's breast and gave up her own heart to him. He had not imagined she would do that—his own solution had seemed so obvious—no, certainly her actions were not at all what he would have done. But then, he had never imagined anyone might feel pity and mercy for a darkangel, let alone love. Only when Aeriel lay down among the ashes on the floor and closed her eyes did he come to himself and realize he must be quick about it if he were to save her.

Lifting a lamp from its niche in the wall, he brought it over to where she lay. He knelt down beside her and felt the air just above her lips for breath—her breaths still came, but very faintly now. The dram of life, her wedding toast, was keeping her yet alive in the world, just barely. As for the one who had been the vampyre not an hour before, his breaths were coming deeper and stronger all the time.

The little mage of Downwending picked up the lump of lead from the floor and held it above his lamp's white flame. The cold lead grew warm and soft in his hands. The outer coating ran and dripped away. The duarough nodded. There was still living flesh underneath, as he had hoped. Why had the girl not thought to do what he was doing now? The little man pursed his lips. Love did seem to have a way of dampening the analytical faculties. He shrugged in agitation, but then softened. Well, who was to say her method might not prove the better?

He let the last of the lead trickle away before he set the lamp aside and turned to Aeriel. She barely breathed. He laid the inner heart of flesh within her breast and rejoined the parted tissues with his hand, grateful for the powers yet lingering within the room, surpassing his own poor abilities. Bending over her, he watched anxiously. Soon, gradually, the color crept back into her face and she began to breathe deeply again. He settled back on his heels to wait.

WHEN AERIEL OPENED HER EYES, SHE saw the duarough sitting on his heels to the side of her. She raised herself a bit, and looked at him in wonder. "How is it that I am not dead?" she asked him softly. Unease overcame her then as she realized what that might mean. She glanced about her worriedly. Had the little mage somehow undone her doing, given her her own heart back and let the darkangel die?

"Peace, daughter," her companion assured her. "He lives. I have given you the vampyre's heart." Aeriel touched her breast, felt her fear subsiding into puzzlement. The duarough continued, "It was lead without, but flesh within. I have removed the lead and given you the flesh. How do you feel? Are you well?"

Aeriel nodded. Indeed, save for a little weariness, she felt better than she had in many daymonths. "The darkangel," she said. "How is he?"

"No longer a vampyre," the duarough answered, "nor icarus—and well enough. Come look. He is about to wake."

Aeriel sat up slowly and waited for the world to steady, then leaned closer to look at the one who lay beside her. His wings had fallen all to feathers that lay like scattered leaves beneath him. The slashes on his face and shoulder had closed over now in clean, pale scars. That he was but a youth surprised her. He looked little older than herself.

Despite the scars, he was very fair to look at, much fairer, she realized, than the vampyre had been. His skin was the light, dun color of the plains people and his hair was as glossy black as Eoduin's. He stirred once, as in troubled sleep. His eyelids fluttered. Aeriel watched, and when his eyes came open then, she saw they were as blue as earthshine.

"Nurse," he cried, sitting up stiffly. "Dirna, I've had a dream." His voice, though husky, a youth's, had somehow the quality and inflection of a child's. He sat a moment, frowning anxiously, murmured as to himself, "A long and wondrous dream..." He caught sight of Aeriel suddenly and started. "Who are you?" he asked.

Aeriel told him her name. "What did you dream?" she said.

"I remember...," he began. "I dreamed I was a vampyre who drank maidens' blood." He halted, perplexed, looked at Aeriel more closely. "You were in my dream," he said. "But I do not know you. How could I dream...? And Master Treasurekeeper," he exclaimed, catching sight of the little man beside her, "what brings you to my chamber at such an hour?"

"We came to kill the darkangel, my prince," the mage replied.

"You are Irrylath," said Aeriel suddenly, quietly. The realization at once surprised her and did not. "This castle, then, is Tour-of-Kings."

"I am Irrylath," he replied. "My mother is Syllva the Queen, and my father is the chieftain Imrahil. Maid, are you some new lady of my mother's? Where is Dirna, and my other attendants?"

"What did you dream of Dirna?" asked the duarough gently.

The young prince thought a moment. He shivered as with cold. "I dreamed," he said, "I dreamed that Dirna pushed me into a still, dead lake and I lay on the bottom amid the eels' nests and the water weeds a long time very cold until a lorelei found me and brought me to her palace."

Aeriel felt a second understanding steal upon her. "The vampyre's lorelei and the Fair Witch of Dirna's tale are one," she murmured soft, very soft beneath her breath. Now she understood the desert jackals and their pursuit of her for the im-mortal hoof.

"There she cast spells over me," the prince continued, "to cause me to forget my name, and taught me all things new—how to strangle little marsh hens and...and other things." He closed his eyes a moment, shivering. Aeriel wrapped her arms around herself. "She used to sing to me at night," said the youth. "She told me she was my mother, and in the dream I believed. The lorelei said that when I was old enough, she would make me a vampyre to join my six brothers and conquer the kingdoms of the world."

He opened his eyes, looking at nothing. As Aeriel listened, his voice grew strained.

"Ten years passed while I was with her in her palace. Then one night she gave me a dram that was very cold, and drank off my blood that the cold would not kill me, and opened my breast with her fingernail to gild my heart with lead." Aeriel laid her hand on her own breastbone even as the prince touched his. "Then she gave me a dozen great wings and told me to fly and find a kingdom, then return to her in fourteen years with the souls of as many maidens for her.

"So I flew home to Tour-of-Kings, which was

my own father's castle, though I did not know it—but my father was dead and my mother gone away across the Sea-of-Dust. Then I stole and married fourteen maidens in as many years." The furrow between his brows deepened. "But the last one poisoned me." He turned to Aeriel. "She looked like you." Aeriel could think of no reply. He looked away from her again and chafed his arms. "Such a terrible dream," he murmured. "I've taken chill from it, I think—my voice sounds different this morn...."

The duarough shook his head. "No dream, my prince."

The youth looked at him, then glanced about him uneasily, at Aeriel. Then he shook his head and made attempt to laugh. "No, surely you are sporting with me. All is as it was when I retired, I...went to bed. I went—is it morning yet?" His words had slowed, but quickened now. "I must rise early, for my mother and I are going on a pilgrimage to Lonwury...." He stopped himself again, shifted. "Or...but—I have already been to Lonwury. We stayed a year. And then in the desert, Dirna woke me.... I, or was all that, too, part of my dream?"

"Look at yourself, my prince," the mage replied. "You are no longer a boy. Look at the scars

on your face and shoulder. Hear the deepened timbre of your voice. This castle is deserted. There
rests the chain the lorelei gave you. The dust of
maidens lies scattered on the floor, and there burn
thirteen new-made stars in heaven."

Irrylath gazed about him slowly. He had fallen
utterly silent now. Aeriel saw him flinch at the
sight of the dust and the chain and the night-dark
feathers on the floor. His movements had altered
subtly, grown weightier, and as he gazed, his face
grew ashen-colored when he put one hand to his
throat where the chain had been. He felt one
shoulder blade, no longer winged, traced the new-
healed scars upon his cheek. His back stiffened.

"I remember," he murmured, letting go his
breath. His voice trembled. "It, then—all of it was
true, and not a dream." He turned suddenly on
Aeriel, sat staring at her. "I have lived ten years
with the lorelei, and these last fourteen a darkangel." He caught up a handful of dust from the
floor and watched as the fine grey stuff slipped
through his fingers. "I have murdered"—he
blinked, swallowed as against great dryness—
"worse than murdered thirteen maids. I remember
it." His voice had hoarsened to a whisper. He
looked up from his empty hand at Aeriel again
"I would have murdered you."

The tremor in his voice distressed her. She felt her own heart twinge with his pain. "Courage," she told him; "peace," and reached to touch his hand. "You are not the darkangel anymore."

But he shuddered at her touch, started back as though she stung. "I am," he cried. "I have been."

Then Aeriel, too, drew back. "What's this I've done?" she murmured, gazing at him. "It was not solely your body I meant to heal."

He shook his head. "Why have you spared me?" he whispered. "I don't understand."

Aeriel struggled; no words seemed enough. "There was a little good in you. You let me feed the gargoyles, spared the bats, and then my own life more than once."

Irrylath closed his eyes. "Not kindness," he said. "Surely I never meant any of it for kindness."

"Even so . . ."

"Children," the duarough interjected then, his tone gentle and reproving. The young prince started, as though he had forgotten the little mage entirely. Aeriel was slower turning to face the duarough. "Children," he said again, "mercy or love cannot be earned. They are free gifts only. This maiden's merciful love has made a start at healing you, my prince. Who knows what it will accomplish with time? And that is well. But just at present, I think, we must turn ourselves to more pressing matters."

"The lorelei," said Aeriel.

"Just so," the mage replied.

"She must be slain," said Irrylath, his words harsh with hatred. "I must..."

But the duarough was shaking his head. "I fear that may be a bit beyond your power, prince," he said kindly. "Beyond anyone's at the moment, in fact."

"But what can be done?" said Aeriel.

"She will steal another babe and make a vampyre of him when she learns that she has lost me," murmured the prince. His teeth were clenched; his hands beneath Aeriel's were as well.

"And that we must prevent at every cost," the duarough agreed, his tone growing stern, "for when her icari number seven, they will be invincible."

"But there is the blade adamantine," said Aeriel.

"I can wield it," said the prince, catching it up from the floor and eyeing it fiercely, "against the icari. If only I might undo"—his voice faltered

as his gaze fell upon the ashes on the floor—
"*some* of the evil I have helped to cause. Perhaps
then..."

"But how may you ride against them, prince,
without a mount?" inquired the mage.

"Horses are easily come by," began Aeriel.

"But not of the sort he will need, daughter. A
wingèd steed to meet a wingèd foe."

Irrylath's gaze fell. He set down the blade
again. "The starhorse is dead," he answered dully,
"the only wingèd horse in all the world." His
voice grew tight. "I drove him into Pendar to
die."

The duarough said nothing. He seemed to be
waiting. Aeriel sat by the prince a moment in silence. Then she rose and walked to where the
vampyre had thrown down the immortal hoof of
the Avarclon after toasting his bride. She lifted the
silver-bright vessel in her hands and answered
slowly.

"The Avarclon is called undying, yet I saw him
dead. This hoof of his is different from the others.
It shines and does not crumble like flesh and bone.
The lyon called it 'the immortal hoof.'"

The magician laughed his sage's laugh. "Wise
girl," he said, "you have solved even this last
riddle well. You must take this hoof to Esternesse.

There are priestesses and wisemen there with the learning and the science of the Ancient Founders. With their magic and machines, they can restore the starhorse—call back his soul from the center of the world, give him new flesh and blood and bone." Turning to Irrylath, he finished, "In a year's time, he will spring full-blown from his immortal hoof, and bear you against the vampyres in the world."

The young man raised his head. "Esternesse," he said softly, slowly. "My mother is in Esternesse."

Aeriel returned to him. "And you would much like to see her, would you not?"

He turned his haunted eyes to her. "I . . . no— yes," he admitted at last, closing them. "Very much."

"But how?" murmured Aeriel, half-turning. "How may we cross the Sea-of-Dust with neither ship nor sail?"

"Ah, children, but you have a sail," the duarough said, "or the makings of one. And as for ship, I think you will need none."

Aeriel eyed the little mage a long moment in puzzlement, until she saw he was looking at the feathers that covered the floor thickly in the space where the fallen icarus had lain

"My wings," she heard Irrylath beside her murmur, as if new hope were stirring in him now. "The feathers of my wings—there are thousands of them, enough for the weaving of a great canopy."

Aeriel said nothing for a moment. She was looking at the little man. "You will come with us, Talb, will you not," she asked him, "to Esternesse?"

"That I shall not," he replied, "for I've another errand to attend to." He reached for the vampyre's leaden necklace and its charms, tucked them away into his sleeve. "I must bear this to the water witch." His eyes smiled merrily. "I shall tell her, prince, that I am your servant—never mentioning, of course, that you are no longer hers. I shall say that you have bid me bear the tribute to her straightway and you will follow in the morn. She's bound to be growing thirsty. It has been many years since last she had souls to drink."

"But," said Aeriel, "the vials are empty."

"They will not be when I give them to her. I *think* I have fourteen drops left of my distillate— not enough to slay her, or even harm her very much, but enough to give her a bitter taste in the mouth."

"She will kill you," said the prince.

"I think not," the duarough replied, "if I am careful. I am a little bit of a wizard, and I know a trick or two. Well, children"—he nodded to both of them then—"I must be off. And as for the two of you, there is weaving to be done."

Then, before either of them could speak or reach to stay him, he turned swiftly and departed, with never a glance behind.

LATER, IT WAS ONLY MUCH, MUCH LATER that the bards began to sing of the wonders of his journey to the witch's realm—a journey made both over land and under—and of all the marvels that he met along the way. And further, they sang of his disguises, and how he passed the inspection of the witch's many gatekeepers and was at last admitted to her presence. Also of how he beguiled her into drinking the fourteen vials, of her great fury when she discovered his deception, then of how he slipped by her many traps and finally escaped—but all that is another tale entirely. Suffice to say that it was done.

And as for Aeriel and her prince, they wove the whole night through, making a great sail to bear them to Esternesse. Aeriel procured their food from the lighted caves, but they ate in the castle above, for though the stone halls stretched vast and empty still, they had lost their clinging chill. Irrylath worked silently, almost feverishly, beside her, helping her to plait the coal-black feathers. When she could persuade him to talk— and that always low and haltingly—it was ever and only of his childhood at the keep or in Lonwury on pilgrimage. Often, however, when they slept, his cries awakened her. She rose at once and went into his inner chamber to rouse him from troubling dreams. But he would not speak of them to her, and always turned away.

"But time will come," she murmured softly when once more he slept, "that you will not turn from me," and left him again to quieter sleeps.

And when at last the dawn arrived, the two of them took their finished canopy out into the garden, which was beginning to bear fruit again for the first time in many years. Then taking their devisement by the corners, they spread it into the air. The plains wind caught it, and lifted it like a raven sail. The west wind swept them aloft, high over the plains. Far away on one horizon, Aeriel could see the desert of Pendar, and offered a silent prayer for the Pendarlon, that he might by this time be well healed of his wounds. In the other direction, she caught sight of the mountains of Terrain, at whose foot her village lay. Before them lay the Sea-of-Dust, and beyond that, Esternesse.

And just as they crossed from over the plain to above the sea, they heard far away in the distance behind them, a hideous cry. It came, Aeriel realized, from the depth of the dead lake on the desert's edge, and embodied all the raging hate she ever could have imagined, and more.

"The witch," she heard Irrylath behind her breathe, "she has discovered the duarough's trick, and that I am lost to her."

"Talb," said Aeriel, listening to that furious scream, "I hope he slips safe away. If she should take him..."

But her companion shook his head. "No," he answered quietly, with the first hint of calm, true hope she had heard from him since his awakening, "I think we need not fear for him."

The scream of the white witch rose louder, shriller, and ended in a shriek that caused the very air to shudder. Then, as its echoes rebounded from the steeps and gradually died into silence, Aeriel looked up at the sail blown full above them and saw—as the last of the lorelei's magic left it— that it had turned to white. And so on a throw of pure white feathers, she and her chieftain's son crossed over the Sea-of-Dust, alighting later that same day in Esternesse.

Don't miss the thrilling second volume of
The Darkangel Trilogy

A Gathering of Gargoyles

Aeriel's love has transformed the darkangel and rescued him from his mother, the dreaded White Witch. But though Aeriel and Irrylath are free, the rest of Avaric is not.

The White Witch grows ever stronger. Her evil magic blights the land, and her other darkangel sons are growing more bold in their attacks as her power increases. Worse yet, the White Witch has not wholly relinquished her claim on Irrylath—her plans require all seven of her sons, and she will not give up Irrylath so easily.

If Aeriel is to save her world, she must track down and defeat Irrylath's bloodthirsty darkangel brothers—and confront his terrifying mother face-to-face.

"Superb. . . . The author's imagination seems boundless."
—*Publishers Weekly*

Let your imagination fly with the best in fantasy

MAGIC CARPET

BOOKS

The Kingdom of Kevin Malone   (0-15-201191-9) $6.00
BY SUZY MCKEE CHARNAS
Amy finds a magical world in Central Park where bully Kevin Malone is a hero.
Worse still, he needs Amy to save his kingdom and himself. Will she help this
punk she doesn't even like?

Knight's Wyrd   (0-15-201520-5) $6.00
BY DEBRA DOYLE AND JAMES D. MACDONALD
Will Oddosson is told his wyrd—his fate—on the eve of his knighting: He will
meet Death before a year has passed. Soon he is beset by one evil beast after
another. Which will be his wyrd?

DIANE DUANE'S thrilling wizardry series

So You Want to Be a Wizard   (0-15-201239-7) $6.50
Fleeing a bully, Nita discovers a manual on wizardry in her library. But magic
doesn't solve her problems—in fact, they've only just begun!

Deep Wizardry   (0-15-201240-0) $6.00
The novice wizards join a group of dolphins, whales, and one giant shark in an
ancient magical ritual—a ritual that must end with a bloody sacrifice.

High Wizardry   (0-15-201241-9) $6.00
Nita and Kit face their most terrifying challenge yet: Nita's bratty little sister,
Dairine—the newest wizard in the neighborhood!

The Weirdstone of Brisingamen   (0-15-201766-6) $6.00
BY ALAN GARNER
All of Evil's minions are working to stop Colin and Susan from returning the
Weirdstone to its rightful owner, the wizard Cadellin, but the earth's fate
depends on them.

Two fantasy classics by MOLLIE HUNTER

The Smartest Man in Ireland   (0-15-200993-0) $5.00
To prove his boast of being the smartest man in the land, Patrick Kentigern Keenan tries to outwit the fairies. But wit is not much against an opponent who has magic. . . .

The Walking Stones   (0-15-200995-7) $5.00
A wise old man gives Donald the knowledge—and the power—to prevent developers from destroying an ancient mystical circle of stones.

A Dark Horn Blowing   (0-15-201201-X) $6.00
BY DAHLOV IPCAR
Nora is stolen away one night and taken to Erland. There she must tend sickly Prince Elver and avoid the eye of his father, the wicked Erl King, who would have Nora for a wife.

The Forgotten Beasts of Eld   (0-15-200869-1) $6.00
BY PATRICIA A. McKILLIP
Sybel's only family is the group of animals that live on Eld Mountain. She cares nothing for humans until she is given a child to raise, changing her life utterly.

Tomorrow's Wizard   (0-15-201276-1) $6.00
BY PATRICIA MacLACHLAN
What's wrong with Tomorrow's apprentice? Can he not hear the High Wizard's warnings? Or is it that the apprentice would rather be a human instead of a wizard?

Are All the Giants Dead?   (0-15-201523-X) $7.00
BY MARY NORTON
To stop Dulcibel from marrying a toad, James must get Jack-of-the-Beanstalk and Jack-the-Giant-Killer to leave retirement and to kill the last of the giants.

The first book in EDITH PATTOU's epic Songs of Eirren

Hero's Song   (0-15-201636-8) $6.00
The trail of his sister's kidnappers leads Collun to a giant white wurme whose slime is acid to the touch, a wurme that Collun must kill if he is to rescue his sister and save his world.

Volume I of MEREDITH ANN PIERCE's classic Darkangel Trilogy

The Darkangel   (0-15-201768-2) $6.00
Aeriel must kill the wicked Darkangel before he finds his fourteenth bride—even though within him is a spark of goodness that could redeem even *his* evil.